Hoosier Woman

A Novel Based on the Life, Times, and Legacy of Miriam Coulter Pence

1865-1917

By Sylvia Freese Duncan

ISBN-13: 978-1475032796

ISBN-10: 147503279X

Dedicated to my Whitley County ancestors, those old settlers, whose integrity and strength inspire and sustain me and, especially, to four preceding generations of strong Hoosier women. I hope to do them honor.

Ancestry Leading to the Author

Elizabeth Jenkins married William Coulter
George / John / Evan / James / Margaret (Sis)/
(unnamed infant) / Frank/ Orlando / Miriam /
Mary / Willie

Miriam Coulter married David M. Pence
Evan / Lilah

Lilah Pence married George McConnell
Helen / Marjory (Marjorie)

Marjorie McConnell married Karl Freese, Jr.
George / Sylvia

Sylvia Freese married Thomas Duncan
Andrew

Foreword

This book would not have been written had it not been for a very unusual artifact: a black hairpiece made of human hair and carefully preserved with century-old, dried flower petals and tobacco leaves in a long, flat Adam's Black Jack Gum box. It came into my possession many years ago from my mother, along with several other items that had been carefully preserved and handed down from her grandmother Miriam Coulter Pence. The additional relics I have of this woman include: a yellowed photo of a young, but dour, Miriam wearing the curly hairpiece; an exquisite quilt (pictured on the book cover) fashioned by her mother in 1870; a leather-bound New Testament carried from Ireland to this new land in 1809 by Miriam's grandfather; her 1882 *History of Whitley and Noble Counties*; and a most intriguing medical book entitled *Dr. Chase's Receipt Book and Household Physician* with notes and recipes penned in her own hand and attached to the pages with straight pins. This medical book gave proof to family lore that Miriam stepped out of the traditional role of farmwife and rode side-saddle to tend to her greater community the best she could. She utilized both Dr. Chase's modern advice and the knowledge of herbal medicines handed down to her by her mother, who was an early settler in the wild land of northern Indiana less than a decade after the Miami and Potawatomie Indians were forcibly removed from the Indiana Territory. The land was subsequently meted out to white settlers who came in droves to stamp their marks of ownership on the dark, fertile, mucky ground laid down by the glaciers and overgrown with deep, dark forests of hardwood trees; cranberry bogs; and clear, clean, spring-fed natural lakes.

I am a born and bred Indiana woman, who succumbed to the wanderlust of my ancestors and sojourned stints in Michigan and Colorado. The treasures from my great-grandmother have traveled with me, tucked into a cedar chest and calling to me with muffled voices to tell Miriam's story. I did not know my great-grandmother when I began to write in earnest. I feel we are more than well acquainted now. She and I are family; her blood courses in my veins. She may be somewhere in the Great Beyond chuckling, or in outrage, at the fictional license I have taken with her thoughts and words, but as I did my historical research, poured over cemetery records, and studied my aunt's memoirs, I gained insight every day. Her story transported me into new and exciting places in the history of my family and gave me a true appreciation for my ancestors' cherished sense of place on Indiana soil.

My intention from the start of this

project was to create an engaging story for the current and future members of my immediate family in order to help them understand the legacy of the preceding generations. As I progressed, I discovered a remarkable thing. Each of us has lived, or is living, a life worth remembering. We and our ancestors do not need to be famous, or infamous, in our time to still have fascinating stories to tell of joys, sorrows, challenges, losses, and victories.

Miriam is real to me now. I cannot fit into her size four shoes, but I can weep at the gravesides as her little brother, father, and mother are laid to rest. I can be in the congregation and rejoice when she is united in marriage to a good man, and I can stand in awe at the bedside as her second granddaughter, my own mother, is born. I have walked and ridden with her through some of the days of her life on this earth. I can honestly say I love her—this woman who was a stranger to me when I, in wonder, carefully lifted that hairpiece from the box and heard her voice speak clearly to me, "Sylvia, tell my story because it is yours, as well."

CHAPTER 1 1870

Her consciousness swam up from the depths of sleep. She heard a faraway, plaintive, "Halp! Halp!" Her heartbeat quickened as the sound became more immediate and urgent. "Halp!" With a start, she surfaced and opened her eyes to the early dawn light. Her nose was cold and the ropes on her bed frame complained as she pulled the red and green appliquéd quilt around her ears and snuggled deeper into her down mattress. A sleepy smile lighted her face as a door closed and muffled footfalls passed by her room, and she suppressed a giggle at the familiar commotion on the landing. Pa was fussing again. "Liz...those dang peacocks! I swear one of these mornings I'm gonna shoot 'em, pluck out their purty feathers, and Tildy can cook 'em up for Sunday dinner. To sit straight up in bed every morning to the sound of a child's cry just fries me! I'm an old man with five young-uns at home and a soft-hearted, critter-lovin' wife. All this is bad for my ticker! You hear me?"

Miriam listened to her wonderful, strong father stomp by on his every morning routine, her little bed vibrating to his steady footfalls, but, suddenly, she heard him stop, turn back, and he stuck his head into the small room she shared with her sister Margaret, ten years her elder. His eyes sparkled with warmth and mischief. "Rise and shine, birthday gal! I suddenly remembered and I'll bet you remember, too. Five years old and you aren't married yet, are you?" He rushed over, pulled down the quilt, and tickled her ribs until she squealed with pleasure. His hands were rough and gnarled but extra good for tickling. "How is my dark-haired Irish beauty this lovely morning? Lounging in the bed, I see. Up, up! Day's a wastin'. I can smell those buckwheat cakes cooking already. Tildy isn't wasting any time this fine morning."

"Hey, Sis. Top o' the mornin' to my big gal, too!" He turned to the second bed in the room, leaned down and gently kissed the top of Margaret's head, her long dark brown hair in a tangle visible above the blue and white woven coverlet. She emerged from her warm bed into the chilly room and responded with a teenage yawn and stretch. Sis was fifteen and thought of her little sister as her pretty doll to dress and tuck in at night. Then, when she finished playing, she left Miriam to her own devices, putting her doll in the corner. Sis's long, slender, ivory arms and her creamy complexion were the envy of her little sister. Pa danced a clumsy, little sideways jig on his way out of the room. He loved to show off for his girls, but even in this early spring season—too wet to plow—morning chores could not wait. They never waited—summer, winter, spring, and fall. He chose this life, and farming could not be done halfway.

Miriam wiggled her bare toes on the wide tulipwood plank floor. Brrr! Her nightgown of linsey woolsey was getting too short for her, but Ma was busy making her a nice cotton shorty for when the hot and humid Indiana summer returned. She remembered watching her mother at the spinning wheel and loom creating her nightgown by hand. Ma had shown Miriam how to prepare the loom with thick linen thread and to weave the softly spun lamb's wool through the linen—the shuttle clicked back and forth as the fabric seemed to grow like magic before her eyes. As Sis ran a brush through her hair and began to dress, Miriam hopped over to the window and looked out at the early spring morning. A skiff of snow lingered around the garden plot and in the shade of the outbuildings. The pie plants her mother sometimes called rhubarb were bravely thrusting their wide leaves above the fertile soil, and their arrival completed the comforting cycle Miriam was just beginning to notice and to embrace with joy. She was glad her birthday came when the earth was beginning to turn

green.   Her family was hankering to
celebrate after the long, cold northern
Indiana winter.

Miriam watched as her older
brothers Evan, James, and Frank slogged
through the barnyard puddles in the boots
they painstakingly waterproofed by the
fireplace the night before. Sitting on her
weary Pa's lap in the flickering light with
her dolly in her arms, she had watched the
big boys quietly labor over the warmed,
dark brown leather, twice rubbing in the
greasy mixture of beef tallow, rosin, and
beeswax.   Those precious, glossy pairs of
boots sat side by side on the hearth all
night, just as the boys walked side by side
this morning. The largest of the peacocks,
eager for his breakfast and a little mischief,
raced over on his long legs, and Frank gave
him an ornery, petulant kick to keep the
bird from flying into his face.   Miriam
cringed and a little storm crossed her
birthday face. The menfolk in the family
sure hated those birds, but they didn't dare
lay a finger on them in their mother's sight.

Miriam shared her mother's passion
for birds: noisy roosters, clucking hens, and
the geese and ducks that splashed in the
creek and made a ruckus in the barnyard.
Pa said you didn't need a dog to warn
about strangers on the property, if you had
geese worth their salt.   Guinea hens

scampered, squawking, as they scratched the earth and snapped up grubs and grasshoppers all the day long. Ma loved her peacocks and peahens. The parlor's crowning glory was a tall cut glass vase from the factory in Warsaw filled with cast off, iridescent peacock feathers in shades of green, purple, and blue with mesmerizing eyes at the widened tips. Miriam knew Ma's story well: peacocks were especially made by God to bring the rainbow to their home place each day. Ma said that her own mother had kept peacocks on the farm in Ohio, and she taught her an Irish blessing to go along with their loveliness. Miriam stood with her belly pressed up against the windowsill, and her breath created a mist on the glass pane as she looked out upon her whole world and whispered:

"Wishing you a rainbow
For sunlight after showers—
Miles and miles of Irish smiles
For golden happy hours—
Shamrocks at your doorway
For luck and laughter, too,
And a host of friends that never ends
Each day your whole life through!"

How fine her mother was–better by far than any other mother she had met at church or spied on her rare trips into the general store in Churubusco. Ma loved the wild birds, too, and taught Miriam to recognize the song of the scarlet cardinal, the scolding of the blue jay, the cawing of the mischievous crows, the liquid warble of the robin, the mimicry of the gray catbird, and the echoing gobble of the wild turkeys that grew fat on their many acres of fields, woods, and hedgerows. The boys suffered from her edict that they were not to shoot the song birds or the owls...or even the pesky crows or wheeling buzzards, though their trigger fingers itched to use their black powder rifles on anything that moved. Deer, yes, when the larder was bare, and the ugly, tusked wild pigs that roamed the woods rooting up acorns were fair game for the boys. Miriam had overheard the neighborhood men speak about her pa and her brother Evan as the best wild game hunters in Whitley County. A smokehouse full of hams and venison was something to be very proud of and to depend upon during the harsh winters—even, upon many an occasion, to share among less-fortunate neighbors and church friends.

Beyond the barn stretched her father's pride and joy: large fields of well-drained, coal-black, Indiana loam claimed from the hardwood forest by back-breaking work. Trees were girdled, burned, or felled by the axe and crosscut saw; stumps were pulled by straining oxen. Slash burned, flamed, and smoldered day and night in all seasons for more than two decades. When the last walnut trees were transported to the sawmill, the oak and hard maple split and dried in the woodpile, the team of oxen sold, and the smoke from the last brush pile cleared, the plow, pulled by a pair of young, muscular Norman horses, sank deep into the virgin topsoil and ran along as smooth as you please: no rocks, no roots, no mortgage.   Her father, roughened hands and sunburned face, cried out with pride, relief, and joy.   Ma told Miriam that the whole family had rushed into the barnyard worried by the sound coming from the field.   They thought Pa was in trouble. As they rounded the house in a panic, the boys looked toward the fields and recognized this was the moment they had been struggling to achieve—the sight they had waited to see since the day their Pa sat them up on the broad backs of the oxen to ride home from the fields and forest after they had given him their best effort—even better than their best.   George, Evan, James, and Frank stood tall, their heads held high, as they heard Pa bellow joyful commands, "Gee!"and "Haw!" to the powerful animals as he reveled in this rich land—660 acres he had beaten into submission to produce a vast harvest of corn, wheat, hay, wild game, domestic livestock, and fuel.   He, William

Coulter, yeoman farmer, grandson of Ireland, first generation American, a man of land and means, would build a rich life for his wife and children in this territory that had been swept of the Miami and Potawatomi just seven years before his arrival with his wife and two year old son George. He, and hardworking family men like him, were the rising tide and the future of this nation. For twenty-three years he struggled to wrest this land from the wilderness. He and the five boys, doing men's work, with the grace and help of God, had tamed all but 100 acres into farmland, twenty-eight acres of cleared forest a year. Many families could only manage to clear six or seven a year, but his four oldest were caught up in his passion to work the soil, and they became magnificent young men in the white-hot crucible of back-breaking toil. They were sons of unquestioning loyalty.

The untouched acres were reserved for a woodlot for fuel and hunting, a sugar bush of beautiful hard maples, and a wetland that brought flocks of migrating birds by the thousands in the spring and fall: the majestic great blue herons; comical, rattling kingfishers; and the savory wild ducks that graced the Coulter table. His young wife seemed to need contact with the birds and beasts of the forest, marsh, and barnyard in order to find beauty and meaning in this isolated, developing country, short on the finery and time for the friendships he had asked her to leave behind. His dear Elizabeth, seventeen years his junior, a mere slip of a girl of eighteen, had supported his desire to leave their well-established lives and family down on the banks of the Ohio River and to follow the lure of free land in the newly surveyed and established State of Indiana. She, barely out of childhood herself, at his side in the covered wagon, had rumbled northerly along dirt roads in the year 1847, and they had moved their belongings into a small log cabin prepared in advance for them by a neighbor on their wooded homestead. His father, John, had made the necessary arrangements to secure promising acreage and adequate shelter on his first scouting foray into this new country. William could not resist the promise of his own land, and the fact that cholera was spreading into the downstream villages along the roiling, muddy Ohio River put some haste into their departure. The local doctors encouraged families to flee the miasma and travel inland to find relief from the decaying vegetation and impure water. The Catholic priests swung their incense and claimed that God was punishing the little river towns for their collective sins—a litany that heightened the general level of dread to one of panic. Cholera was hard to treat and often fatal, especially for children and the elderly, and the frontier river towns were in an uproar with the rising epidemic. Why would God send this upon them? Were the diseases of the Old Country going to plague them here as well, just when they thought they were breathing clean, clear American air?

William was thankful Miriam's father had given them a good covered wagon and team and had sent them on their way with his blessing, even though Elizabeth's mother railed against the loss of her daughter and grandchildren. It was as if they were sailing off into a vast ocean in a small boat; the risks were so great and communication with home nearly impossible. It was a heart-wrenching parting, so much so, William had almost lost his nerve, but Elizabeth never faltered in her faith in him. She was his rock. Oh, how he loved this fiercely determined woman.

Over the course of the hardest years, Elizabeth had borne him eleven children. Three of those precious ones were at rest next to the Christian Chapel northwest on the Goshen Road. George was farming his own acres now and raising livestock with the help of his wife Caroline and their two daughters Elnora and Cora. John was married to Ella, a former country school teacher, and they had started a family. Think of it. A third generation, his grandchildren, on this land already. Here, among these people, as the tree roots were ripped from the soil and the native people banished to fend for themselves on the hunting grounds of the western plains, other roots were thrusting their way down—eternal family roots in this great place: Section Six, Smith Township, Whitley County, State of Indiana, United States of America.

Miriam's daydreams dissolved as Sis rustled around in the room. Sis even made Miriam's bed as a little act of kindness on her birthday. Both sisters were happy today. Miriam's birthday brought lightness to the morning—a little something to look forward to for the whole family a break in the daily routine. The girls could already smell the fragrance of birthday cake wafting up the stairs. Miriam had the honor of choosing whatever cake she wanted. She and Pa loved marble cake, and Tildy was happy to oblige because she loved it, too. Yesterday was bread-making day, so today the oven was especially reserved for the birthday girl's cake. Tildy had already hurried the boys through their breakfast and had run them out to their chores. Those big fellows were just trying to get her goat: tromping their newly shined boots around her kitchen. In her domain there would be peace and quiet, no slamming doors and fallen cakes. She was an important part of this family and had come with them all the way from Ohio as a sixteen year old, just two years younger than the missus. The missus had never learned to cook and fuss with housework, so the mister had hired her to help with those tasks and the babies, too. She was thankful for the roof over her head and the kindness of these people. She was one of thirteen Irish children in her family, and there just hadn't been enough food to go around. She was a big, red-headed, freckled girl among these slight, dark-headed folks. Anyone could sure tell she wasn't a Coulter, but she was loved and respected just as if she were a cherished sister. She had assisted at the family's childbirths, had bathed and tended the thriving children, and had stood grieving at the gravesides of the three babies who had died. She respectfully addressed this man and wife as Sir and Ma'am, just as her mother had taught her, but felt no inferiority in their presence. She had thrown in with this good family, heart and soul, and they showed their gratitude in so many ways as the years of their partnership had gone by. It was love based simply on mutual admiration.

With some help from Sis, Miriam pulled her blue dress over her head. Sis buttoned her up, brushed the tangles from Miriam's long dark hair, braided it, and tied on her gift to her sister: two brand new pink and green ribbons. The chilly weather called for long stockings, too. As they left their room together, Miriam glanced at their mother's closed door. She would be down when she had finished feeding and tending to the new baby, Willie, who had taken up residence in Ma and Pa's room and, worse yet, had stolen Miriam's precious time with her mother. Ma must love him best because she gave him Pa's name. Ma's lap seemed to be always full of Willie, no room for her anymore. It was a lost cause for Ma to try to get her to accept the squalling, scarlet-faced Willie who entered their lives in the dead of the winter of 1869 with only a neighbor midwife and Tildy in attendance. Miriam was appalled that bringing a baby into the world seemed to make you sick; her mother took to her bed for several weeks following, and Miriam was only allowed brief visits to her room. Pa had good reason to hate peacocks, but she had a better reason to hate fat little Willie...even when he aimed his toothless grin her way.

Sis had told her that they once had

another little sister named Mary, who was born when Miriam was only two, but God had taken her from the family before she could even walk or talk and before Miriam could gain a lasting remembrance of her. Tiny Mary, who came too soon, had been a spring baby, too, but died at Thanksgiving time in the same year. Sis said that was why Ma took such good care of Willie. Pa and Sis were in the room when the doctor said his birth was difficult and he must be the last Coulter baby. Well, she guessed if Willie was so important to everyone, she might as well think of him kindly.

Miriam turned up her nose at the buckwheat cakes, and Tildy told her if the birthday gal was so high and mighty, she should get her own breakfast. Buckwheat cakes were common, gritty, and gray. Even the best maple syrup couldn't improve them much. She would prefer a thick slice of Tildy's wheat bread with grape jelly from their arbor, but the boys had stolen the last of the jelly from the cupboard the week before, had taken the quart jar back of the barn, and had sneaked it back into the kitchen as clean as a whistle but leaving telltale, sticky, purple rings around their mouths. Tildy gave them each a swat with the broom, but she had to laugh at their spring craving for sweets. It would be late summer before the Concord grapes would be ready for harvest, and Ma's wild birds sometimes beat Tildy to them. When the grapes dusted over with a white haze and turned sweet and delicious, she had to stake Gyp, the family dog, in the shady arbor to keep the birds and woodchucks at bay. Miriam didn't blame the birds. Last year, Tildy let Miriam stand up on a kitchen chair and very carefully pour melted paraffin in the top of each jelly jar. The deep purple jars looked so pretty lined up in the cupboard.

Miriam settled for a big glass of milk and a piece of leftover cornbread for breakfast. She grabbed her egg basket and a little sack of chicken feed. She pulled on her short woolen coat with the two black buttons. Even the five year old birthday girl had her own chores to do. Her white wrists and hands stuck out of the sleeves shamefully. Pa was right, she really was a growing girl. Pa had installed two rows of coat hooks by the back door. Hers was on the bottom row so she could reach it herself. She sighed and supposed there would be a hook for Willie before very long.

After a cold visit to the outhouse, Miriam yanked open the stubborn door to the chicken coop. Feathers and dust flew as the hens were startled by her intrusion. They dashed around her skirts and out into the fresh air. Biddies scattered at her feet.

She tossed wheat and corn on the ground outside the henhouse, and the hens immediately began their contented clucking, purring, and strutting. Ma had taught Miriam how to deal with their feisty rooster, who was eyeing her from the dark corner of the coop. Every day since he had been a chick, Miriam had been picking him up and handling him gently. She knelt down and pinned his wings with authority, secured him firmly under her armpit, and began to talk to him and to stroke his head. This protector of the flock, who would fly at her father's eyes with his spurs angled forward in attack, was as docile as a kitten in her arms. His red crest was rubbery and his eyes intense, but he melted in her arms and never struggled, scratched, or pecked her. When she put him down, he raced to rejoin his ladies and chicks. There were a dozen eggs to put in her basket that morning: white, brown, green, speckled, all little orbs nestled in the straw. Ma told her that raising a brood of chicks once in a while assured the family of a constant supply of eggs—goose and duck included. Also, Sunday chicken dinner was a tradition, and Tildy's golden brown and delicious fried chicken was famous all over the township.

Several times a summer, Pa would make a big show of putting on Tildy's apron with the bright yellow bric-a-brac and take a turn cooking Sunday dinner after church. The day before, in the middle of chores, he would holler, "Whose mouth is set for rabbit pie?" and the boys would let out a whoop, put away their tools, grab their guns, and head to the woods and grazing land. Sometimes Pa would go with them and enjoy the day with his boys away from the constant responsibilities of the farm. One time, Miriam even caught a glimpse of them sharing a plug of tobacco as they headed across the field together. When she set out behind them as fast as her little legs could carry her over the clods of dirt, Ma called her back, told her it was man's work. She guessed Ma was right, but she wished she could go, too.

A tired little girl carried her sputtering candle and precious birthday gifts up the stairs that night. Miriam reluctantly untied her hair ribbons and put them in her new keepsake box. She climbed into her bed, settled under the quilt, and recollected the day's happiness. She had unwrapped other presents at the supper table: a small wagon for her doll handmade by Pa; her pretty Easter dress with a lacy collar fashioned by Ma; three beautifully crafted Miami arrowheads found on the creek bed by the boys and presented to her arranged in a wooden cigar box bought for a few pennies from the owner of the general store; and a calico apron just her size made by Tildy.   John and Ella had sent over a cunning yellow sunbonnet, and even George, almost twenty years older, remembered her birthday. He and his family had dropped off a little cameo ring for her. They stopped by for a while, and she got to play with her nieces, who were just about her same age, while Pa and Ma caught up on the news from their house. Her last vision before sleep overtook her was the cluster of loved ones around her tall marble cake frosted all over with sugar icing tinted pink with wild cranberry juice. As she looked around her at the table, the firelight shone on each face, and the love for her and for one another glowed from within. All was right with the world.

CHAPTER 2 1871

On a glorious summer morning, Miriam awakened early and padded quietly across the landing and down the stairs in her bare feet. On clear days, she liked to slip out the front door to sit under the pines without Tildy hearing her from the kitchen and recruiting her to set the breakfast table, so she took care to place her feet carefully on the outer edges of the stairs to avoid any squeaks. It was this time of day when the birds were singing their hearts out for her; the heat of the day hadn't arrived, and she had time to think. Pa stood up for her when Tildy complained that she was just being lazy. He said she was having "pine tree revelations." When Miriam asked what that meant, he said she was working out answers to life's questions while she sat and listened to nature. He said she had caught that fever from him. The fox squirrels and jays chattered to her as she sat on the soft cushion of pine needles and leaned against the rough trunk. She stretched out her legs and studied her stubby toes and tiny feet for a minute. She had to wear soft slippers to church but, otherwise, relished the cool dew bathing her toes each morning.

After a while, Miriam relinquished

her seat, brushed the needles off her bottom, waved goodbye to the curious squirrel that was eyeing her from a low branch, and walked around the house into the barnyard. Her pine tree revelation of that morning was that maybe if she kept going barefoot, her feet would spread out so Pa wouldn't tease her anymore about her "tiny tootsies." She could smell the smoke from the cast iron step stove in the kitchen. Only a few pieces of kindling made a fire hot enough to boil coffee and heat the frying pan to sizzling for bacon and eggs. Tildy would be glad this wasn't baking day—too durn hot to be cookin'—as her Pa would say. Gyp ran up, tail wagging, and she heard the bang of the tin pail, a soft voice, and lowing in the barn. Pa was milking already. Her bum lamb butted his woolly head against the plank fence and gave a plaintive bleat. Pa had given her this orphaned lamb to tend, and it had become her closest companion. Pa cautioned her about giving her lamb a name. He had said, "You are a farm girl and you are getting old enough to understand why we raise animals here. The dog and the cats are the only pets here, Miriam. The horses live their whole lives out serving our family, and they are precious living tools. We care for them lovingly just as we sharpen and oil the plowshares and use neat's-foot oil on the leather harness. We sell the sheep's wool to provide cash for our needs, and we sometimes use their flesh for our table. I want you to begin to think about all these things God gives us as a blessing for our use." She was still pondering these words and what it meant to be a farmer—to till the land, to raise livestock, and to put food on the table, enough for eight hungry mouths. Did she dream of living her whole life on the land? Was there anything else?

Her lamb was old enough now to graze with the flock but still loved to follow her wherever she went. They walked to the clover patch behind the woodshed. The grass had dried there in the sun, and Miriam pulled her spotted lamb down beside her, his head in her lap. Ma had taught her how to weave a garland of clover blossoms, so she braided a fragrant collar for her lamb and a necklace for herself. The green stems and creamy puffs of petals looked so cute around her lamb's neck. He shook his head, flipped his ears back and forth, and capered in a little stiff-legged dance of joy before he ran full speed to join the others grazing on a grassy knoll behind the barn. He wasn't going to need her for very much longer, and that thought gave her pause. Babies sure grew up fast. She glanced at the ground around her. If she had time, she would have loved to hunt for a four leaf clover for love and luck, but she needed to tend the chickens and hurry back inside. Ma had promised to play school with her as soon as everyone else headed out to the fields and Willie went down for his morning nap. Willie had grown nearly as quickly as her lamb in the past two years, and he had become almost bearable. He toddled here and there, and they had to watch him carefully to make sure he didn't touch the kitchen stove. Lately, he had been playing in the sandy lane leading to the barn. He was happy sitting in the dirt for a long time and digging one little hole after another with one of Tildy's cast-off, broken wooden spoons. Miriam couldn't help but think he was a lazy boy. He loved to have everyone "do" for him—feed him with a spoon, carry him down the steps, pull him in a wagon instead of getting hot and tired on his own two feet. Keeping Willie happy and accounted for took a lot of energy from everyone in the family, but he had a bright smile and pudgy little legs and feet.

The family was changing; there was no doubt. Sis was being courted, and she didn't give Miriam the time of day anymore. She was totally distracted by Tobias Aburn, a sandy-haired boy with a fast Norman horse and cart. Ma and Pa liked him, but Miriam could tell they wished she would spend time with someone they knew better. Even if she couldn't find someone of Irish blood, there were lots of Pence boys in the county, who were good German stock from families who were old settlers in the area. There were also Zolman, Krider, and Gradeless boys who were eligible, hard-working young men—some who attended the small Christian Church, too. Miriam thought Tobias was dashing, and she watched her sister blush when his name was mentioned. It seemed like only a matter of time until he would ask Pa for her hand. After all, she was of age and finishing her common school education in the spring.

Sis and Frank were attending school. Ma insisted on it, though Frank spent most of his time playing hooky with two other friends. When Ma and Pa watched him ride off to the township school, they didn't know that the boys often hid their fishing poles in the bushes at the end of the long lane. It was an easy ride to the shores of Round Lake. The fellows would spend their day fishing, swimming, and pulling the wool over Pa's eyes. Pa would have taken Frank behind the woodshed, if Sis would just squeal on him. Sis told Miriam she heard Frank tell Mr. Grable that Pa had hay-cutting that had to be done the next day, so he wouldn't be able to get to school—then he turned around and told Pa that the school inspector was coming by, so he had to be in school for the student count and couldn't help with the hay. Miriam would have told on him, but Sis never did, nor did she tell on James and Evan when they climbed out their bedroom windows to uncover their stash of tobacco and hard cider in the barn loft. Sis needed to keep her brothers on her side, if she wanted to slip out the back door some evenings and meet Tobias at the end of the lane for a moonlight drive. Miriam thought it was shameful the way Ma and Pa were being outwitted by their own brood. Her Ma was like the hen dashing here and there hopelessly trying to keep track of her growing, scampering biddies. Oh, well, as Pa used to tell Miriam when she would whine for help, "I can't do this for you. You must learn to fend for yourself, Miriam." There seemed to be lots of *fending* going on, and she decided just to watch and see what she could learn.

As she delivered her egg basket and its contents into Tildy's hands, she heard Ma call from the rainbow room. That's what the family called the small parlor off the front hallway where the family showed off their best furniture and possessions brought in the wagon from Ohio and a few things they had been able to purchase since coming to Indiana. It was also the clean, quiet space where Ma worked her magic with her needle and thread. She pieced her quilt tops there and sometimes set up her quilting frame, and the ladies from church would come and have a quilting bee right in their house. At those special affairs, Ma's laugh was heard above the whispered gossip and rattling of her few good china teacups on their saucers. A square walnut table with fancy turned legs and a white marble top stood by the front window. On quilting bee days, it would feature a layer cake on a glass pedestal surrounded by flowers from the garden. Today, it held the vase with the peacock feathers glowing in the morning light. The facets in the cut glass threw more rainbows around the room—on the twig rocker, Ma's low sewing chair, the coal oil sconces on two walls, and the horsehair divan that had made a circuitous trip all the way from the factory in Grand Rapids, Michigan, on southbound and eastbound trains and had been hauled by wagon to the house from the Collins station. A small child's rocker sat in the corner. Resting on the chair were Miriam's slate and a piece of writing chalk.

Ma was teaching Miriam the letters one by one, and she was an earnest student. Miriam sat on Pa's lap every evening for his Bible readings, and she was anxious to be able to make sense of the words herself.

She dreamed of reading aloud the McGuffey Readers Evan and James threw carelessly by their boots when they got home from school. As far as she knew, Frank was the only one of the boys who read these marvelous possessions, but she often sat in the corner by the back door and looked at all the pictures in these books. Liz recognized a kindred spirit in Miriam. Her daughter demonstrated an unquenchable desire to learn. She mastered the bird names and sounds with such ease. Four of Liz's children showed no interest in book learning, so she wanted to kindle the sparks she saw in this young daughter. She recognized that John, too, was blessed with a good intellect and married a wife who valued learning, but she was fighting a losing battle with William over the younger boys' educations. William felt his seven years of common school didn't teach him anything compared to what he had learned by the sweat of his brow. He believed the true tests of manhood showed in the calluses on your hands, the pedigree of your livestock, and the bright eyes and strong arms of your sons. He claimed their oldest, George, who had only three years of book learning, possessed all the skills needed to make a great success in this country. From his toddler days, George showed a natural, almost uncanny, way with horses, and he worked slowly and knowledgeably to build up the most elegant breeding stock of Normans in the county. He relied on his capable wife and daughters, if any reading or writing needed to be done, but he was highly respected, honest as the day is long, and gaining substantial wealth. On the way home from church, they would often see the neighbor men hanging on George's fence admiring the beautiful, glossy animals and imagining with what ease they would pull the plow and the wagon. Seeing those men and George doing a little horse-trading on the Sabbath seemed shameful to Liz, but it made William very proud.

Miriam's daily lesson began. Ma printed a capital letter, and Miriam traced over it. Then she formed the letter on her own. After Ma approved her letter, Miriam erased the slate with a wad of raw wool and handed the slate to Ma. They invented a funny game thinking of things that began with the letter of the day, and Ma wrote the words spelled correctly for Miriam to study. "D is for dye, dog, door, doctor, dress." When Ma wrote "dandruff," they shared a laugh and a hug. If real school were going to be like this, Miriam was going to love every minute.

When Pa and the boys came in for their midday dinner, Tildy was ready for them. The four hungry fellows sat at the table and passed the basket containing thick slices of whole wheat bread and hot cornbread, and they dug into slices of smoked ham. The green beans were fresh from the garden. Tildy had simmered them all morning in water seasoned with bacon grease, salt, and pepper. There were steaming buttered new potatoes in their jackets, and, to top it all off, strawberry shortcake with a dollop of fresh sweetened whipped cream. Willie toddled into the kitchen, climbed onto Pa's lap, and suddenly planted his face right down into Pa's shortcake. He came up grinning with whipped cream from ear to ear and a big strawberry in his mouth. Even Miriam had to join the laughter. She had to admit, he had a certain charm. Pa predicted he had a bit of the leprechaun in him and would live a golden life.

After lunch, Pa announced, "My nail keg is empty. Evan, hitch up the horses to the wagon. Who wants to go to 'Busco?" A dozen chair legs scraped the floor, and Frank's chair purely flew as he made a mad dash up the stairs to his bedroom, followed by the rest of the children. Even Tildy's eyes sparkled at the rare chance to go to town and to make a few purchases at the dry goods store. The Coulters gave her a small allowance above her room and board, and she liked to send her mother and father a little remembrance once in a while. Ma headed to the backyard pump, stripped off all of Willie's clothes until he was as naked as a jaybird, and pumped cold water all over him from head to toe, washing off the lingering shortcake and the layer of dust from his play in the barnyard. He squalled to beat the band and tried to wriggle his wrist from her iron grasp, but she persevered until the water ran clear. She swept him, dripping, into her arms and headed upstairs to dress them both for town. Pa never went to town in his overalls, so when Miriam had combed her hair and put on her newest dress, she met him striding across the upstairs landing—spring in his step and smile on his face. His hair was slicked back and he had on his church clothes. She adored her Pa, the most handsome man in the county—maybe even the world.

CHAPTER 3 1871

By the time Miriam and Pa got out to the barnyard, the boys had hitched up their handsomest horse to the light wagon. The rumbling, cumbersome covered wagon the family used to move their belongings to Indiana was stored in the barn and still in use for heavy farm work: delivering hay to the threshing machine, taking great bags of wool gathered from the neighborhood in shearing time to the water-powered carding machine on the St. Joe River north of Fort Wayne, hauling logs to the mill and split wood to the woodpile. This lighter one-horse wagon with red wheels was purchased with some of the proceeds from William's ten year crop—a memorable anniversary year when God graced the county with abundant sunshine and just enough rain, and William had been able to plant and harvest eighty acres of high quality corn. He found this conveyance useful for supply trips to Columbia City and Churubusco and for transporting the whole family to church. He needed a family wagon that would take the bumps easier on Liz, who was with child most of the time, it seemed. Having a stylish, light wagon and a well-groomed horse showed the neighbors he was a man with some extra money in the bank and a little leisure time on his hands after two decades of struggle. The sleek black Norman horse had been a generous Christmas gift from his son, George, whose high quality strong and gentle horses were well suited for driving, saddle riding, or the plow. William had been a great help getting him started in a business that had made his reputation, and George was always quick to show his gratitude.

Sis helped Tildy into the wooden box bed and handed Willie up to her. Sis and the boys piled in the back, and William lifted Miriam and Liz up onto the plank seat. The leaf springs made Miriam and her mother bounce a bit as they settled in for the ride. William gave the horse a good word and a gentle pat and climbed up with the reins. Off they went down the long lane to the Goshen Road, the most improved road in the county for which the residents were very grateful. Before this hard dirt road was built, it was tough going in a wagon. Older settlers, those bold and determined men, had told him stories of how they had to ford swollen streams and squeeze through the dense forest. It took three hard days to get to Fort Wayne, the only place to buy supplies at the time. He shuddered to think about bringing a family here in those dangerous days. William knew he and those who had come in response to the land rush twenty-some years ago couldn't hold a candle to those intrepid men and women—that great generation of brave families who first opened up this wilderness for them all. He felt in his bones those old starvation days were over forever. He tried hard not to be prideful of God's blessings on William Coulter, the Scriptures were firm on that, but he and Liz sat up straight and proud. This wagon rolled along just as smooth as you please.

The whole family fell silent, each mind drifting to the slow rhythm of the turning wheels and the hypnotic clop of the horse's hooves. Willie dozed on Tildy's lap, and the boys lounged against the wagon sides, dreaming of the treasures they hoped to see in town and reveling in the precious time away from work. Miriam admired the way Pa had cleared, trimmed, and manicured their lane. Now that the fields were tamed, the process of fencing had begun, and splitting fence rails was a never-ending task that mostly fell to the boys. James, at nineteen, seemed to take satisfaction in the work and could be trusted to head to the woodlot and make a good showing for himself without his father's supervision. His arms and back were muscled and lean. His hands were as rough as Pa's.

One special fence line had been created by weaving a row of planted hedge apple, or Osage-orange trees. Cuttings were taken from a tree down by the creek and stuck close together in single file in the fertile ground. During the first few years, Pa bent and twisted the branches to interweave the thriving little saplings. After five or six years, the tangle of branches that resulted could stop even their biggest workhorse in its tracks. This natural fence harbored many birds in its twisty branches and, in the fall, dropped dozens of rock hard, bumpy green fruits on the ground. The boys loved to throw them at each other. A well thrown hedge apple—the boys called them horse-apples—would raise a nasty bump when it landed on a boy's thick skull and sometimes would leave a nasty rash from the milky sap. Ma would gather a few, slice them, and let them dry under the stove into pretty forms that took the shape of flower petals. She used her plant dyes to stain them shades of red, green, and orange and fashioned them into holiday wreaths for the neighbors. She tossed a few of them around the perimeter of the house to ward off bugs, too. Pa whittled the hard wood to reveal pleasing shades of cream, orange, and chocolate brown. The Miami tribe prized the wood of the Osage-orange for their fine hunting bows, and Pa still treasured the bow he had fashioned for himself when he was a boy in Ohio. It was strong and supple and he kept his boyhood bow-hunting skills sharp on rabbits and squirrels. He always told his children they would not starve in the wilderness if they could catch a fish, shoot true with a bow and arrow, and harvest cattail roots and wild cranberries from the bogs.

They headed east at a leisurely pace. There was no hurry on this beautiful day. Pa loved to get out and take note of the improvements his neighbors were making on their farms. He took great pride not only in his own acreage but in the quickly improving property of others. Settling this land took teamwork, sharing, and friendly relations with most everyone, even a few of those ornery old settlers and those naïve men—new to the area and to farming. He had once been considered a "mover," and he knew what small kindnesses had meant to him and his wife and son upon reaching their homestead. The Egolfs brought a spicy hickory nut cake the first week when he and Liz were overwhelmed and, to face it squarely, scared. They were thankful to find a church home. At first, there were just a few people gathered together, but now the congregation was growing and trying to do good works.

The neighbors recognized his God-given skills in negotiating the inevitable disputes that came from wandering livestock, shared property lines, and growing pains of this new part of the country. He was committed to neighbors living in peace and harmony with each other and the land. He had not been criticized for his boys' avoidance of service during the War Between the States. People knew the Coulters didn't have any interest in politics. He tried to be generous to the wives, children, and widows left behind from that terrible conflict that had shed the blood and crippled the bodies of many fine men and boys from Whitley County. Many others had never returned from battle but were buried where they fell in Kentucky, Tennessee, Virginia, and Alabama. He fervently prayed at the end of each day that peace would reign and allow the United States to heal, to go on with its great expansion, and to provide opportunities for his children and all his progeny long after he was resting in Indiana soil. He gazed about him. On his right, a new barn stood in whitewashed elegance next to a tidy frame house; on his left, calves frolicked and head-butted each other like little boys playing tag. The corn was growing so fast you could almost hear it—crisp dark green leaves unfurling in the summer sun. In the distance to the south, a misty haze rose over Blue Lake. One of these days he wanted to take Miriam to catch her first fish. He had just finished fashioning a fishing pole and was hiding it in the barn for the right moment to surprise her, to saddle up, and to whisk her off to the lake. He knew she wished she could go with him on his hunting forays with the boys and was disappointed to be left behind. Maybe a day with her pa could lessen the sting. She was such a dear girl.

Miriam studied Pa and the faraway look in his eyes. She wished she knew what he was thinking. Whatever it was, it was wonderful and made her happy to see him so relaxed. She turned and looked at her mother. Ma reminded her of the queens she had seen in the McGuffey Reader—sitting straight, shoulders back, dark hair peeking from under her best green bonnet, the ribbons tied in a loose bow under her chin. Her fair skin wasn't tanned and burned like Pa's. Instead, she had a smooth face with just a hint of crinkles around her bright eyes. She had told Miriam they were called "crow's feet," but she would rather call them "smile lines." Ma felt Miriam's gaze, smiled, put her arm around her, and drew her snugly to her side.

Before long, they started to meet

more and more people on the road. It was fun to wave at everyone and to get a friendly greeting in return. Drawing near to town was exciting, and soon the first buildings came into view. The boys began to stir in the wagon bed. Willie stood at the side and beamed at everyone they met; the mothers gave him a special smile and wiggled their fingers playfully. Mr. Zumbrum, on horseback, hailed Pa and told him to bring the family by their place after church on Sunday. It had been a long time since they had a good visit, and he wanted to talk about putting their money together to bring the thresher closer to home this year and combining their corn harvest to get a better shipping price. Pa turned to Ma with raised eyebrows, and she happily nodded her assent. Pa assured him that Mrs. Zumbrum could count on their visit.

Ma said she needed to stop by Ross and Mager's drugstore, so Pa pulled into a space between buildings, put a feedbag on the horse, and announced to everyone that they should meet back at the wagon before too long. "When I give my whistle, you come arunnin', okay?" The boys said they were heading off to Richards's dry goods store to look around and then to watch the men building the new hotel down by the depot. Miriam went with Tildy and Ma to the drugstore and then to look at fabric. Pa hoisted Willie on his shoulders and set off to Henry Pressler's hardware store for nails and the news. Henry had his finger on the pulse of Churubusco and surrounding parts and always had time to step out from behind the counter and visit. Afterward, Pa would take Willie by to watch the sparks fly in Jim Witham's blacksmith shop and then introduce himself to a newcomer, Robert Hood, who had just built a new wagon shop in town. He needed axle grease and thought he would throw some business his way—cash on the barrelhead. It was nice to have someone close by who could true up a wheel.

Unless you needed a bank, you could do about all your business in Churubusco any more. He heard the strident whistle of the steam engine as the train approached town. He strolled down the street to give Willie the thrill of hearing and seeing the Detroit, Eel River and Illinois train chug in and come to a lumbering, squealing halt at the depot and discharge its passengers and cargo. My, oh, my. How this county was growing. There was Doc Squires to take care of your illness or broken bones; Doc Palmer to fix your teeth or pull 'em out; Bill Shifler could order you a ring for your gal's finger or fix your pocket watch. The new United Brethren Church was going up in town, and travelers were going to have a nice place to stay when John Deck got finished with his hotel. Whooee! What a bunch of movers and shakers, and he and his family were an important part of it all.

Chapter 4 1871

When Miriam skipped down the stairs in the morning, Tildy bustled from the kitchen and shushed her, index finger over her closed lips. During the night, Willie had developed a high fever and sore throat. The parlor, handier to the kitchen and more isolated from the bedrooms, had become his sickroom. Tildy took care to keep the kitchen quiet as she simmered clear vegetable broth, brewed weak peppermint tea, and filled a basin with tepid water and a bit of cider vinegar so the missus could give Willie sponge baths to bring down his fever. Word had come from church that several of the children had contracted scarlatina after last week's services, and the doctor was out making rounds to the houses.

Ma sent Frank to find the doctor and to have him come as soon as he could. Usually milder than full-blown scarlet fever, scarlatina was what took her toddler Orlando away from Liz seven years before, and she was frightened. He had been just Willie's age when he breathed his last in her arms and God claimed His little angel. Orlando, her fair haired, blue-eyed boy's memory came flooding back. She could not let that happen again. During the war, there had been no doctor to send for, and she and Tildy felt helpless as Orlando failed despite their best efforts and desperate prayers. Surely now, with that conflict long settled, the doctor would bring a modern day cure—perhaps some of those new sulfa drugs. Doc would tell her that Willie was going to be all right—just the ague, or a developing case of chickenpox. A tear slipped down her cheek as she whispered, "Please, God. Don't take my dear son."

Miriam was not allowed in the sickroom, so she sat outside under her pines, listened to her birds, and prayed for her little brother. She felt guilty. Maybe some of her early jealousy of this brother had brought this on as a punishment. Through the open window, she studied the firm set of her mother's lips and the furrow in her brow as Ma and Tildy whispered, heads together, and Miriam knew this was serious business. Ma had employed all her nursing skills learned from almost thirty years of childrearing. She had given Willie an emetic to empty his stomach and a laxative to empty his bowels. She knew that was the first thing the doctor would ask if she had done in anticipation of his visit. Ma put everyone on notice that the house needed to be quiet morning, noon, and night. The windows were thrown open in the parlor to let in lots of fresh air and sunshine for the patient. Willie would cry about his sore throat for a while and then sip some broth; she would bathe him, and he would have a spell of restful sleep. That was a hopeful sign. Ma sat in her sewing chair next to the sleeping couch that had been made up for him. Tildy would watch the mantel clock and spell her at the top of each hour, so Ma could rest a bit and keep up her own strength with some solid food and water, but, after ten minutes, she was always back again at his side.

Miriam watched the doctor come up the lane in his buggy. He smiled and waved at her and carried his bag in the back door. She tiptoed to the window and sat under it to eavesdrop on the sickroom. After all, Willie was her brother, and she had made up her mind she would protect and love him every day of his life. This was her pledge to God, if He would allow Willie to get well.

The voices in the room were muffled, and Miriam had to listen very carefully. Pa, Ma, Tildy, the doctor, and Willie were in the room. It was very quiet until Willie began to groan and whimper. The diagnosis was scarlatina, and the doctor haltingly spoke in low tones to Ma and Pa that one of the neighboring children was dead from the malady already. He assured the stricken adults that all hope was not lost, however; he would do all that was possible. He administered leeches behind Willie's ears immediately and gave him foxglove as a diuretic. To Ma's great disappointment, he didn't have access to any miracle drugs. He instructed Ma to continue her lukewarm sponge baths until the fever broke. Tildy would have to leave food outside the parlor door. He declared that Ma was going to have to be confined to this room and shoulder this whole burden. Tildy gathered nightclothes and a chamber pot for Ma. Miriam and the rest of the family were to stay away, and Tildy had instructions to keep every utensil and dish scrupulously clean.

Ma and Willie battled the disease for a full week. Miriam and the family fretted outside the parlor door and the window. They watched Ma's drawn face with dismay. Willie didn't cry anymore. He was too weak from the fever that Ma didn't seem to be able to bring down. She could barely force liquids into Willie's inflamed throat. His tongue was bright red and his chest and arms looked sunburned with rash. His breathing was irregular and labored. The church women quietly brought baked goods, but they mostly prayed. They had just buried two babies in the churchyard, and they knew how much this little boy meant to Liz. She had confided in her women's church circle that Willie was to be the last Coulter child. The doctor had told her that her childbearing years were over, if she wished to live to see her youngest children grown. She had lost three of her last six children. In tears, she asked her women friends and God why her first five children had all lived despite the lack of health care and the isolated conditions, but she had lived through such personal tragedies with the last six, beginning with the child who only lived six days and went to the grave, unnamed. The women all knew of Miriam's suffering and guilt over that baby's death because it had been reported in all the papers. It seemed that the coroner was called to make too many tragic visits to the Coulter home, and this instance was the worst. The baby had arrived during a terrible cold spell—way below zero day after day. It was too dangerous for the doctor to be on the road, so the baby was delivered with the help of William and Tildy while the other children huddled by the fireplace and listened, wide-eyed at their mother's cries. The baby arrived into an icebound world. The livestock were suffering and school had been closed. Everyone stayed indoors and tried their best to keep warm in their insubstantial houses with only fireplaces, kitchen stoves, and down coverlets on the beds to ward off death from exposure. The bedrooms were so cold. Liz and William invited Evan and James to share the bed with them and the baby to keep warm. On the sixth night, the baby stopped breathing sometime during the night. Whether the infant was smothered under the bedcovers or whether its death was caused from a weak constitution from birth, they would never know. The county paper got hold of the story from the coroner, and a reporter wrote a poignant piece that touched the hearts of everyone but brought shame to Liz as a mother. The neighbors, and even those at church, had looked at her in pity, but she saw a touch of accusation in their eyes that broke her heart. William was furious at the invasion of their privacy, and Liz was still struggling with guilt. Should she have stopped bearing children then? Was it a sign from God she had ignored? Her two closest woman friends were empathetic listeners. They had both walked in her shoes and knew her heartache firsthand. They comforted her with the thought that Frank, Willie, and her dear Miriam were put on this earth to do God's will, and they would not have been born, had she quit desiring children. Her living children were healthy as could be and still needed her, but, they advised, she and William should heed the doctor. She would not be of service to God or to her family if she ignored his warning and tragedy ensued.

At the end of the long first week of October, Miriam awoke early. It was still dark. The house was silent. The new mantel clock was not ticking. Tildy was not bustling about the kitchen. Something was very wrong. She tiptoed down the stairs in her nightgown and saw the door to the parlor open. Shadows moved slowly, as if underwater, in the light of the oil lamp. She walked to the door and peeked in to see a tragic tableau. Ma and Pa sat at the foot of the sleeping couch. Pa's arm encircled Ma. Their heads were bowed as if in prayer. Tildy stood behind the bed. Willie lay still, the flush gone from his cheeks, a peaceful expression on his face. Slowly, Tildy bent down and pulled the sheet up and over Willie's face. What was she doing? Miriam cried out and ran to her mother. She knew she wasn't supposed to be in the sickroom, but what were they doing to her Willie? He was her responsibility…she had promised God, Himself.

For two days and nights, little Willie Coulter lay silent in a cherrywood casket in the parlor. He was snugly fit into the coffin crafted on his day of death by George and John in John's workshop—both men in deep mourning while building a coffin for their brother. They had always stepped forward to perform this task; the first time they were barely in their teens. They had put hearts and souls into each of four little boxes down through the years, and they worked quietly to skillfully plane the wood, cut the dovetails, and fashion the handles. As a finishing touch, John had carved a lamb resting in a bed of clover on the lid. Ma lined the coffin with a piece of ivory taffeta she had been forced to borrow from Miriam's trousseau. Later, she would buy several yards of white cloth for Miriam's wedding bonnet and use the remainder of the ivory fabric to make pillows for the children in remembrance of their brother.

During the wake, a member of the family was always in attendance in Ma's sewing chair. Evan and Frank spelled Ma and Pa during the nighttime hours so they could get some needed rest. The clock pendulum hung lifeless; all the mirrors in the house were covered. Tildy had drawn all the curtains in the house. As was tradition, a window in the parlor stood open. Neighbors and church friends stopped by for short visits to express their sympathy. Fearful at first when she was ushered in to see Willie, Miriam had, afterward, been emboldened and spent some time studying his little body up close. She thought he had a familiar expression as if he were drifting to sleep in his father's arms. He was asleep, at rest, and Miriam finally understood the expression she had heard Pa speak from time to time: "Rest in peace." That was truly what Willie was doing. He would be tucked into the earth as if into a warm, welcoming bed. His light hair was washed, dried, and combed into wavy bangs over his high forehead. He was dressed in a white cotton shirt with a rounded collar and a pair of brown woolen knickers fastened at the knee. He had on long stockings and soft satin slippers. His waxy ivory hands rested at his waist and grasped a sprig of orange bittersweet berries. His mouth drooped in a relaxed pout, his eyes slightly open. Miriam memorized every detail. So this was death.

A funeral procession transported Willie's body to the churchyard for burial. Families arrived at the Coulter farm, and the boys unhitched the extra wagons and put the horses out to pasture. Families dressed in somber colors packed four large wagons. Ma and Pa drove George's black buggy hitched to his finest black gelding. Willie's coffin rode on the platform in the back. Four other wagons followed…horses plodding slowly all the way. The minister emerged from the brick chapel to meet the mourners, Bible in hand; the little grave stood open and waiting. George, John,

Evan, and James served as pallbearers and carefully lowered the little casket into the grave. As everyone gathered around on a beautiful fall day, the minister said a brief prayer, giving Willie's soul in safekeeping to his Father in Heaven, and then his rumbling voice began a familiar hymn.

Everyone who was not overcome by grief joined in, and the cemetery rang with voices. This hymn summed up all they were thinking, and tears streamed down even the rough faces of the farmers in their black hats and church coats. Pa was stricken, and Miriam looked up through her tears and saw that he seemed to be getting old before her eyes. But he roused himself, as if suddenly inspired, and sang with gusto; his clear tenor voice soared over all the others and rang out to the churchyard, where the horses lifted their heads and pricked their ears:

"O God, our help in ages past,
our hope for years to come,
our shelter from the stormy blast,
and our eternal home.

Under the shadow of thy throne,
thy saints have dwelt secure;
sufficient is thine arm alone,
and our defense is sure.

Before the hills in order stood,
or earth received her frame,
from everlasting thou art God,
to endless years the same.

A thousand ages in thy sight
are like an evening gone;
short as the watch that ends the night
before the rising sun.

Time, like an ever-rolling stream,
bears all its sons away;
they fly, forgotten, as a dream
dies at the opening day.

O God, our help in ages past,
our hope for years to come,
be thou our guide while troubles last,
and our eternal home!"

CHAPTER 5 1872

Miriam had been ready for this day for a long time. She was finally going to school. Ma and Tildy would be left alone at the house while Evan and James were in the fields, but when she expressed concern about leaving them to fend for themselves, they patted her head, smiled, and assured her they would try to carry on without her the best they could. Being a schoolgirl didn't preclude her chores, however. She and Frank had to rise in the dark to get their work done before Mr. Egolf stopped by in his wagon to pick them up at the end of the lane. This new revolting development foiled Frank's hooky-playing, but the weather had turned chilly soon after the harvest, and he and his buddies had the whole winter to figure out how to skip school in the spring.

Mr. Egolf and his pretty wife were raising a bunch of lively school-aged children, and, as the designated trustee, one of his responsibilities was to help the schoolmaster stoke the big pot-bellied woodstove in cold weather. He was charged with making sure the schoolhouse was kept in good order and the stern schoolmaster, dressed always in his black suit and who peered soberly over his wire-rimmed glasses, was a passable teacher and a capable disciplinarian. Mr. Egolf was glad someone else was doing the teaching. The teacher earned room, board, and very little extra. He was expected to be a stellar role model for the boys and girls and could not smoke, drink, frequent the barber shop, or, God forbid, enter a billiard hall. He boarded with a farm family and rode his horse to school each day. The trustees had been fortunate to find a man who had stuck with the job longer than usual, so Mr. Egolf did his best to keep the dour bachelor happy. Mr. Egolf had never had the chance to learn to read or write, but he was following his eldest girl's progress, and she sometimes read him the stock report from *The Columbia City Commercial Mail* when an occasional copy came his way. His wife was pleased to hear Lucy read aloud, too, especially the articles about some of the women's societies springing up in Columbia City. Since Columbia City was way too far to travel for something as trivial as a ladies' meeting, she would just have to be satisfied with the women's circle at her rural church. Once in a while, Lucy read an elaborate recipe she would try in her humble kitchen, but the Egolf brood fancied plain meat and potatoes.

The student numbers were going to

outgrow this building before too long; Mr. Egolf noticed their little heads were ear-to-ear as they leaned over their slates. Plans were in the beginning stages to add an ell for some of the older students, who were good at helping each other with their studies. The state had just begun taxing folks to help pay for the schools. It made plenty of the neighbors hoppin' mad to be taxed on their property value, but Indiana had put this law in place, and this seemed to be one of the costs of progress. There were bound to be plenty more taxes coming, the way the state was growing. The fellows down to the legislature had knock-down drag-out battles and shouting matches over it, but the result was a small, but steady, stream of income for the trustees to manage wisely. Mr. Egolf figured to let them fight it out, and, meanwhile, he was thankful for his children to move forward beyond his own level of book learning.

Miriam had her slate and required books ready. She couldn't sit still long enough to eat much breakfast. Tildy packed her tin lunch bucket with a biscuit and grape jelly...her favorite. Frank accepted the responsibility of looking out for his little sister on her first day. He could be a mild-mannered boy and would rather be fishing than watching over her, but Miriam knew he would fight like a tiger if anyone tried to harm her. He took her hand and they walked together down the lane in the dawn light. The bumpy ride to school was fun with the Egolf kids hollering at the top of their lungs, singing, and hanging out of the wagon on all sides.

Miriam was proud of the schoolhouse. Along with the other men from the neighborhood, her Pa had helped build it. Pa had even hung the double front doors that could be swung wide open, when they expected a crowd. She had been in the school many times in her young life. It was a central meeting place that served the community well. A spring party celebrating the graduates featured square-dancing and tables groaning with potluck. The schoolhouse was made of logs with puncheon floors. The imposing cast iron stove roasted those students unfortunate enough to be seated close to it. The walls were chinked with mortar made of clay. Four expensive glass windows, generously donated by the people of Miriam's church and proudly installed by Pa, let in lots of light, and the furniture consisted of a sufficient number of indestructible backless benches, more conducive to backache than to comfort. The schoolmaster directed Miriam to her spot on one of these benches. The writing surface in front of her was a broad slab, planed smooth and supported by stout pegs, or pins, driven into auger-holes in the walls, and she ran her hand gently over the surface where she was proudly going to show prior knowledge of her letters. Miriam was finally going to officially learn reading and writing. Ma said she could go to school without any knowledge of arithmetic, geography, and grammar, so Miriam's head was as empty as her slate concerning whatever those subjects were. Ma told her that students were not organized in classes except in reading and spelling. If she wanted any difficult point explained, she had to wait until the teacher was at leisure, raise her hand to be recognized, and then stand up and go to him at his desk to ask her question. Ma offered to always help her on her home assignments and would make sure she was ready to compete in the spelling bees and recitations.

Miriam's life soon fell into a pattern of chores, school, reading her schoolbooks by the fire, Pa's Bible lesson, and then bed. Sure enough, Tobias asked for Sis's hand before the holidays, and they planned to be married the next spring. Pa had lined a poplar chest with fragrant red cedar for Sis's Christmas present, and Ma had contributed thread and some fabric. Ma and Sis were working very hard on her trousseau—embroidered linens for the bed, two quilts, and a comforter filled with goose down. Brass candlesticks and an oil lamp sent from her grandparents in Ohio were wrapped carefully and nestled among the linens. Ma's parents were going to be coming to the wedding. It would be their first visit to the farm, and there was lots of excitement. Pa teased that he would just as soon put them up in the hotel in Churubusco since they had never warmed up to a man in his thirties wooing their teenage daughter. Ma gave a laugh and told him he had better be good because her parents would be sleeping in his bed, and her mother would be treated like a queen, or he better get used to the idea of sleeping in the shed with the milk cow. His bemused expression made the whole family roar with laughter. Finding himself suddenly the center of attention, Pa, with booming voice, launched into his favorite poem about the old settlers, "In the immortal words of the great poet R. H. Stoddard:

Men married women then
Who kept their healthful bloom,
By working at the churn
And at the wheel and loom;
And women married men
Who did not shrink from toil
But wrung with sweat their bread
From out the stubborn soil."

He ended his recitation with a flourish of his hand and a deep bow to the applause of his audience. The firelight played on all their faces. Sis blushed. At some point she was going to have to tell her family that she and Tobias intended to go west to Iowa after their marriage.

CHAPTER 6 1876

Miriam awoke from a terrible nightmare. Pa called out to her, but she couldn't see him in the dark, and her feet wouldn't move; something held her back, clutching at her ankles. He needed her, but she remained helpless, paralyzed. She began to struggle and to call out his name. It was hot, so very hot. Miriam bolted upright. She looked around her in the darkened living room as she gasped for breath and felt her hammering heart. A tear ran down her face as she remembered. Pa was ill, so very ill. The doctor had come last night. Frank had ridden down the lane full speed at dusk to summon him from Churubusco. He arrived in his black buggy, lantern swinging, around midnight and disappeared into Pa's room. Miriam felt her world crumbling when she saw the doctor's grim face. She huddled with her five brothers who had been summoned and who had all assembled by the fireplace. After several hours, Ma had come downstairs for a pitcher of water; her sad eyes and drawn face told them the tale. It was bad. She ordered them all to get some rest, so they gathered blankets and slept downstairs, close together for comfort.

Miriam was only eleven. She was too young to lose the light of her life, the man who had always been so strong and encouraging. She remembered their summer fishing trip; he and she were all alone on the banks of the lake in the still morning air. He whooped and carried on when she managed to hook and land a fat catfish, and they had cooked it up for shore lunch right then and there. She could still conjure up the fragrance of the bacon grease and the taste of the crisp cornmeal and flaky white flesh. Such an ugly critter on the outside, but, oh, so wonderful on the inside. She told Pa all she had learned in school that week. He always took an interest in her doings at school, but instead of the irritable man at the blackboard, who freely wielded his hickory switch on the bad boys, Pa was really the man who taught her the lessons of life. He taught her how to be brave and strong and to stand up for herself against her overbearing brothers. She learned a lesson about a father's love when he gave his blessing to Tobias and Sis as they set out to try their hand at a different sort of life, but he also assured them that Sis was to be the owner of sixty-two acres of good land, and she was welcome to come back to it whenever she wished to return home. That much land could give them a good start until, with hard work, they could afford to add more to it. He understood the desire to establish their own place; after all, that is what he and Ma had done, despite some protest from her family. He would not stand in their way.

How would she ever find a man to love like she loved her Pa? She remembered reading about women who never married. That was the answer. She would go into one of those dark, shadowy cloisters she had read about, where all she would do from dawn to dusk was pray and bake bread. She would ask her Sunday school teacher about how to find one of those places. She prayed to God, pleading for her father's life. Ma explained Pa was sixty-seven years old. He had labored forty of those years as a proud farmer, and Doc seemed to think his heart was just worn out from so much hard use.

She threw off her blanket and quietly tiptoed up the stairs and across the landing to her parents' room. The door was open a crack and she stuck her head in. The doctor was listening intently to Pa's heart, and Pa smiled at her. He didn't seem to be in pain. Her voice breaking, she rushed across the room and into his arms, "Lounging in the bed, I see! Rise and shine! Time's a wastin', Pa."

He gathered her in his arms and kissed the top of her head. "Miriam. You must listen to me. Your Ma needs you now. Sis and the boys are all going their own ways, or will be very soon. You must know I am not leaving you because I want to, but I can hear God calling me home—and we must always obey God's commands. Doc is a good doc and he is telling me true. The angels are coming to take me with them. I can hear them singing, and they have given me their word they will bless you and keep you all the days of your life. I won't be here to see your graduation or to meet the man you will marry, but I command you to make the most of your life, and you will meet me again on the far shore some day. Take care of your mother until the day when she comes to be with me. Do you understand me, Miriam?" He closed his tired dying eyes, and Doc ushered her out of the room. Miriam knew there would be another wake. She went to her room and sobbed into her pillow so no one could hear.

The churchyard was filled with buggies, wagons, and saddle horses on a beautiful fall day as the community gathered to witness William Coulter laid to rest in the Indiana soil he loved next to the church he had faithfully attended. Sis sent word that she could not come. Her first baby was due any day and funds were tight. Miriam could not believe she would miss her father's funeral. She was angry Sis had left home and rarely sent word. Ma was burying Pa here in this land they all loved just as another life was entering the world in a place unimaginable and far away. It seemed to Miriam that this must be God's plan in the United States— everyone was to move westward in a great wave, pushing the Indian nations ahead of them, while Pa's body rested next to his four babies whose souls had entered Heaven before him. Frank and Evan prepared one of their father's favorite hymns for the graveside service and raised their voices in a duet that surprised and pleased the mourners, especially Ma, who knew Pa was listening:

" Jesus, keep me near the Cross,
There a precious fountain.
Free to all – a healing stream,
Flows from Calvary's mountain.

In the Cross, in the Cross,
Be my glory ever;
Till my raptured soul shall find
Rest beyond the river.

Near the Cross I'll watch and wait,
Hoping, trusting ever,
Till I reach the golden strand,
Just beyond the river."

Afterward at the house, tables were fashioned from wide slabs of lumber from the barn and stumps from the woodpile. Tildy supervised as the ladies laid out a funeral supper on their best serving dishes. Miriam and her mother retired to their rooms to rest in grief and exhaustion. Miriam found it impossible to sleep, but she was glad to escape the crowd. Sometimes subdued laughter broke out among clumps of the men and boys—the sound chilled Miriam to the bone. There would not be a time for laughter ever again. She could not get shut of the anger and loss she felt, and she didn't have anyone to share her feelings with.   She prayed all these people would just go away.

But they didn't. She wanted to honor her father's memory, so she washed her face at the basin in her room and rejoined the gathering. After the ladies fawned all over her, hugging her to their ample bosoms and whispering their sympathies, she took refuge in the henhouse. A dusty ray of sunlight slanted across the floor, and she stood in it, hugging herself, to warm her chilly bones. A new clutch of biddies peeped and hopped in one of the nests, and she held one to her cheek and felt its downy feathers, warm and comforting. Suddenly, a pair of dark eyes peered through the slats in the coop, and a boy about Miriam's age shyly walked in the door, stooping a bit because of his height. He looked self conscious and awkward, his wrists and hands hanging way out of his sleeves and his ankles showing. He had neglected to put on any socks under his brogans. He had an almond-shaped face, deep-set eyes, ears that stuck out, and a prominent nose. She didn't recognize him from school, and he wasn't one of the boys from church, but he, too, picked up a chick and handled it gently. "I'm sorry about your pa," he finally said quietly in an uncertain voice. "My pa said on the way over that he thought your pa was the best farmer in the county, and I always believe his word. I saw you come in here, and Pa said I was supposed to give my condolences to Mr. Coulter's children. I hope I'm doing this right." He ended his little speech with a sheepish grin, and, before she could respond, he replaced the chick, turned on his heel, and silently disappeared out the door. He moved like an Indian, even on those big feet. For the first time in weeks, Miriam smiled as she considered that shy, dark-headed boy. She thought he had done it "just right."

Ma had still not joined the gathering, so Miriam quietly crept up the stairs and peeked into her room. Ma sat by the window looking out through her precious lace curtains upon the scene below. She motioned to Miriam to come over and, too big for Ma's lap, Miriam pulled a low chair over so they could sit, knees touching. Ma fingered something in her hands, and, without saying a word, she smiled, nodded, and placed the object in Miriam's outstretched hand. It was a little rock, carved from a smooth greenish stone in the shape of a bird at rest and warmed by her mother's hands. The curious object filled Miriam's palm, and she turned it round and round, inspecting it in wonder. "Miriam, in your hand is a birdstone—one of Pa's favorite possessions. It tapped his ankle on his first pass of the plow on our homestead, and he always contended it jumped up to bless us all. The ancient people who used to roam this territory as part of their hunting grounds left this behind as a reminder of their existence thousands of years before the Miami and Potawatomi Indians, recent tribes you have learned about in school. These ancient ones moved across this very farm—maybe even camped here, gave birth to their babies, bathed and played in the Blue River, and raised some crops in the summertime. They hunted the deer and other animals of the forest and then, sometime in years long ago, disappeared to a place unknown."

Miriam closed her fingers around this precious object. She held a little bit of Pa right there in her hand, and the stone's warmth brought her a sense of comfort. A tear tracked its way down her cheek, and Ma leaned in to wipe it away with the handkerchief tucked into her sleeve. Ma wanted Miriam to keep the birdstone. The boys would inherit other personal things: his rifle, bow, and some of his good woodworking tools, but she felt Miriam, with her love of the birds and of her father, would cherish this memento far more than any of the other children. She asked Miriam if she remembered Pa had told her she would need Miriam more than ever. Miriam silently nodded. She and Miriam held hands as they walked into the barnyard, and the women surrounded them in their protective embrace. Ma and Miriam surrendered to their loving care. Miriam felt the birdstone still warm and comforting in her pocket. She carried it the rest of the day and tucked it safely into her keepsake box at bedtime.

CHAPTER 7 1880

Miriam was quickly becoming a young woman, and she and Ma came to depend upon each other, just as Pa had wished from his deathbed. The farm was divided. Each of the five boys inherited eighty acres. Ma retained the original home and 136 acres, which Frank, James, and John kept farming just as their father would have done for the benefit of their mother's income. Miriam received title to sixty-two acres that her brothers would farm for her until her marriage, giving her a nest egg from her profits. Sis and Tobias had returned with their children and established a home to the east of Ma's house on the sixty-two acres given to Sis, but re-registered in Tobias's name. Miriam could not accept the hurt caused by Sis's lack of closeness during her time away. It was no wonder they had not succeeded in Iowa. The house they built was cramped and untidy, the children poorly clothed and often unsupervised. When time for school came, Ma had to badger them into sending the girls, and Tobias loudly and constantly complained about the taxes on land that he had been freely given. He was benefiting from the hard labor and commitment of her

Pa, and Miriam held a grudge. Ma had taught Miriam to be strong, but Sis had obviously not learned that lesson. Miriam cringed when she heard Tobias order Sis about as if she were the hired help—worse—a slave. It was all Miriam could do to be civil to Tobias and Sis, though her heart went out to the children.

Miriam moved on after Pa's death even though she had a hole in her heart that was difficult to fill. The discipline of school helped to ease the pain of her loss, and she threw herself headlong into her studies. Science interested her the most, and when James offered to take her to see the "big doin's" in Wabash, she jumped at the chance. They would take the train down and could stay with the McNallys, who were family of church friends because there would not be any hotel rooms available in town.

The little town of Wabash, population of only a couple hundred souls, was expecting 10,000 people to descend upon it as it attempted to become the first electrically lighted city in the world. The city council had been coping with the town's growing pains for a while; Wabash was the county seat and its crowning glory was the courthouse in the town square. It had been proved that lighting in a village or city made the streets and sidewalks safer for pedestrians and horse-drawn vehicles. The council was wrestling with the issue of whether to install traditional gas lamps on the corners, which necessitated hiring a lamplighter to go around each evening to do the lighting and the maintenance, or to go out on a limb with the newfangled idea of electric lighting that a fellow named Edison had been working to perfect. The leading men did some investigating and discovered that a man in Cleveland, Ohio, named Charles Brush was working on a new electric lighting system for cities. He was looking for a town and populace to serve as his guinea pigs, and the councilmen said they would be willing to try his invention on approval. They advanced $100 of taxpayer money to allow Mr. Brown's lamps to be tested on March 31, 1880. The big event had been written up in every newspaper as far as Indianapolis, and a record crowd was going to be there to either laud the success or laugh at the failure of scientific progress. The town councilmen were beginning to think they might have bitten off more than they could chew. Their chances of re-election, and probably the level of foot traffic in their businesses, depended on this one night. Mr. Stevenson was hoping the seven cigars he had tucked into the inner pocket of his suit coat would serve as lucky charms.

When James and Miriam disembarked from the pleasant train ride into Wabash, they could not believe their eyes. People were pulling into this little town in every sort of conveyance, and the place was abuzz. They said hello to Mrs. McNally, dropped their bags in her vestibule, and then hurried off to study this contraption before it got dark. The project was to emanate from the courthouse, and they were swept along by the jostling crowd that filled the streets. Four big lamps hung from the flagstaff on the courthouse lawn. Each of the 3,000 candle lamps was backed by a galvanized iron shield. Two telegraph wires could be seen running from the flagpole to the courthouse roof, and bystanders told James and Miriam that the wires ran all the way to the basement where the Brush Dynamo Machine was to generate the electricity.

The dynamo machine was powered by an old steam-powered threshing machine engine mounted on wheels and pulled across the courthouse lawn to the side of the building. When interviewed in the papers, Mr. Brush had confidently claimed his dynamo would work as long as the power was generated fewer than 4,000 feet from the lamps. Men stood by to feed split chunks of oak and ash into the thresher firebox. They would have to get a good head of steam built up to power this experiment, and Miriam could tell from their grins and deliberate marching about those chosen few were mighty excited about being part of this potentially historic event.

According to plan, when the sky got good and dark, the courthouse bell tolled eight bells as the signal to start. Excitement was in the air. The steam engine was stoked, the wide belt was engaged and began to fly round and round through the basement window, a switch on the Dynamo was flipped, and a spectacular blinding light streamed down on all the spectators. Men, women, and children all threw their hands before their eyes and cowered from the brilliant white flash. Startled horses whinnied and strained against the hitching posts. Then, with gathering force, a great hurrah arose! A newspaper could be read clearly on the other side of town. The councilmen clapped Mr. Brown on the back, shook his hand in visible relief, and Mr. Stevenson delightedly doled out his cigars as the dozen members of the local band, still reeling from the excitement and partly blinded by the flash, played a decidedly off-key "Onward, Christian Soldiers." The next morning, newspapers around the state and country reported, "For a mile around, the houses and yards were distinctly visible, while far away the Wabash River glowed like a band of molten silver."

After absorbing all the hullaballoo, Miriam and James strolled back through the oddly-glowing streets and long shadows to the McNally's, but no one could think of sleeping after what they had just seen. They sat on the porch with the family and next door neighbors drinking coffee, eating coconut cake, and contemplating what this invention meant for the future. Gone would be the dangers and inconvenience of gas lighting, lanterns, and candles in the home. Before too long, Hoosiers would have wires strung to their houses and barns, even far out into the country. Farmers would work a full day during the harvest and milk late in the evening by incandescent light. No more odors of kerosene or coal oil would pervade the house and their clothes. No tipped-over lanterns that were a fire danger, especially in a barn full of hay. They all laughed when jolly Mrs. McNally remarked she was going to have to buy a whole bolt of velveteen to make new curtains, if they were ever to get a wink of sleep again.

Miriam sat quietly listening to the adult conversation. She was grateful to be an eyewitness to this giant leap forward in the American way of life. Oh, how she wished Pa had lived to see this day.

Chapter 8 1883

Miriam was eighteen. She had graduated from the top form of her school last year and was first in her class, an honor that pleased her mother and brother John very much. She gave a little speech at the end of the year ceremony, birdstone tucked in her pocket as she spoke so she could feel her father's presence. She knew he would be very proud of her.

Shortly after graduation, she was invited to George and Caroline's home for a week. Arrangements were being made for her oldest niece's wedding, and Ma encouraged Miriam to go. Evan would cover her chores at home. Miriam was excited for a change of scenery, and George had a notion that being around their horses might be a way for her to heal. George was suffering from grief at the loss of his father, too. Even though he was almost two decades older than Miriam, he believed he could fill a little spot in her heart where an older brother, old enough to be a father, might be a source of comfort. He also had another idea up his sleeve and wanted time with Miriam alone. He was going to teach her to ride, something their father had never taken the time to do. She needed the pleasure and companionship of a horse, not just any horse, but his best Norman mare, which was gentle as a lamb, loyal, strong, beautiful, and responsive. This animal could be trusted in harness as well as under saddle. He had named her Clover, for the four dark spots converging on her left flank, and, if he knew horseflesh—and he knew horseflesh better than any man in the county—this animal would be a great gift for her. He was anxious to introduce them to one another and see if a spark would kindle between them.

Evan dropped her off at the end of the lane one fine summer morning. Miriam swung Ma's red and green floral carpetbag at her side and enjoyed a leisurely walk past a riot of wildflowers Caroline had encouraged to grow on both sides of the sandy two-track leading up to their modest home. A house-raising party for the bride and groom was scheduled during her stay, so she had packed her nicest cotton dress and light summer shoes. She was preparing to join the Christian Chapel, so she carried her Bible with her, as well. She needed to memorize a lot of verses in the next couple of weeks. She had learned verses both at the log school and in Sunday school, but Ma had not been listening to her recitation lately. Ma explained that it made her sad to not hear Pa read every night, so they had dedicated their evening needlework to preparing a trousseau in the eventuality of her marriage. The boys at church were beginning to buzz around her, but she certainly didn't know why. She hadn't been a very approachable person lately. She wore her hair pulled back severely, her ears prominent, and cloaked herself in a sad and serious aura that couldn't be attractive to boys. The other girls at school flitted and flirted, but she just couldn't do that. It was against her nature, especially since she felt such a heavy sense of responsibility for her mother and the farm. Frivolous play frayed her nerves, and she had to put a rein on her quick temper around her brothers, schoolmates—even Ma. She had never grown much either, so she knew some of her ferocious nature came from watching out for her own interests. She scarcely cleared five feet tall in her Sunday shoes, and her feet had stayed tiny, a size four, despite her prayer that going barefoot as a girl would cause them to grow a bit. Her lips were thin and had no natural upturn like the girls she saw with delicate bow-shaped mouths secretly tinted with cranberry juice when their mothers weren't looking. She despaired inheriting Pa's prominent nose and spent time looking at it from all sides in the mirror when she brushed her hair. Her shoulders and hips were narrow, and her dresses flared out from a small waist. Even though her toes were stubby, her fingers were tapered and graceful. That always puzzled, but pleased her. Better to have stubby toes one could hide in shoes than stubby fingers for all to see. She wore her cameo ring on the pinkie finger of her left hand and a locket hanging from a thin gold chain around her neck.

She had inherited her mother's eyes. They were dark brown under naturally arched brows, and, when at rest, they looked deep into the souls of others, but, when angry or challenged, they snapped with a cool ferocity. Anyone speaking to Miriam knew what she was thinking because she could not hide her emotions. Sadness showed in her eyes, happiness, too, and anger flashed like lightning. Friends and foes alike had learned to read her well. She had become an outspoken young woman, and it would take a special man to appreciate her, for better or for worse.

George shouted a hello from the barnyard. She waved back and met Caroline at the door. She was a wonderful sister-in-law, sweet and welcoming. Their house wasn't as grand as Ma's, but it suited their little family of four, and, as Miriam looked around, she saw it was simply furnished and tidy, with a splash of color here and there and a charming braided rug at the hearth. John's long rifle hung as decoration above the mantel. A few pewter plates and mugs graced the built-in cupboard next to the kitchen. Elnora called from the attic loft, and Miriam climbed the sturdy ladder, pushing her bag up in front of her. A third cot had been made up for her, and the three girls shared an excited hug at the pleasure of a girls' holiday, of sorts. A person could only stand straight up in the center of the loft, and Miriam, in her haste to unpack, knocked her head on one of the beams and fell back onto her cot in amazement. She laughed at her clumsiness and the girls joined in. This was going to be fun, if she could manage to stay in one piece.

The next morning broke bright and cool. The girls had giggled and visited until their candle sputtered out and were slow to arise to their chores. Miriam helped Cora gather her eggs, being sure to make a fuss over their beautiful white Leghorns. The old rooster flew into Miriam's face, and she retreated quickly from the henhouse. What a crotchety old bird. She was glad she had taken the time to tame her rooster. Maybe this one was past taming, but she would try to show Cora how to get him under control while she was here. George invited her to go with him into the paddock, and the other girls trailed along. They seemed to know a secret and were stifling giggles with their hands. Elnora and Cora climbed up onto the fence and rested their heads and arms on the top rail. Their eyes were shining with mischief, and Miriam was puzzled why she had been left standing in the middle of the paddock all alone, until she turned to see George leading a striking mare from the barn. This was no run-of-the-mill plow horse; she was an amazing animal: young, strong, and light gray with a few dark speckles on her broad rump. Her long ivory mane cascaded over her neck, and Miriam could see that it had been washed, braided, and then brushed into soft waves. Her tail reached the ground. This shining horse obediently entered the enclosure, and George began to exercise her at the end of a long lead rope. She glided around and around in long smooth strides and responded to George's every command. Miriam couldn't take her eyes off of her, and an occasional toss of Clover's head let Miriam know that the horse was eyeing her intently, as well. Clover seemed to be showing off for her as Miriam turned, turned, turned, her feet pivoting in the dusty, well-trampled earth.

George finally brought Clover to a halt, and the horse walked right up to Miriam and put her head down, inviting a pat on the nose. Her dark eyes twinkled with curiosity as she met this quiet girl for the first time. Clover spoke with a gentle whinny, and George interpreted. "Miriam, Clover is trying to say, 'Top o' the morning to you.'" Mesmerized by the horse's size and beauty, Miriam barely had enough breath to whisper, "Top o' the morning to you, Clover." A girl and a horse. A horse and a girl. George grinned because he knew at that moment he was witnessing a match made in Heaven.

During the next few days, George and Miriam could be seen on horseback all over the neighboring farms and the dusty roads. She was struggling to find her seat on a side-saddle that George knew would please her mother. He had seen a few women ride astride in manly-looking pantaloons, on a western-style saddle, but it certainly wasn't the way a modest young woman from a good family should ride. Perching precariously on this powerful animal was strange and scary; Miriam felt vulnerable and very high off the ground. She tried her best not to look down. Learning to climb into the saddle provided the greatest challenge. She had fallen backward into George's arms twice and once onto the ground—rising up in an undignified tangle of dusty skirt and petticoats. Each time, Clover stood stock-still, craned her head around to calmly regard her exasperated rider, and patiently made sure Miriam dusted herself off and tried again.

Riding side-saddle required a good sense of balance in order to protect both herself and Clover. George gave her good instruction, and she was determined to be worthy of his generosity. At first, she required some help to secure her left foot in the stirrup, to pull up onto the saddle, and to place her right leg correctly over the pommel, arranging her skirts the best she could for the sake of modesty. George told her that since both of her legs were on the same side of the horse, there would be a tendency to put too much weight on one side, which could cause harm to Clover because Miriam would have to cinch the saddle too tight. She had to learn correct posture and to sit squarely with her spine centered over Clover's spine. He gently turned her shoulders to the right to center her torso and showed her how to hold both reins squarely to the horse, keeping them at the same length and tension. George said he would show her how to let the gentle Clover know her wishes without having to wear a spur on her left boot. He could only spare this old side-saddle for Miriam. Perhaps she could get a better one later. But, for a beginner, he liked the way the stirrups could be adjusted for her, and the saddle was a good fit for Clover's broad back. He showed Miriam how she could use her right leg, draped over the pommel, to keep a good solid seat and encouraged her to point the toes of her right foot and to relax into Clover's movements. Good posture, balance, and coordination were needed to master the side-saddle. He handed her a light riding whip, three feet long, and explained she would need this to gently cue Clover's right side in place of her leg. He cautioned her to carry her hands high in order to best communicate her wishes to her horse. After Miriam gained confidence, she felt elegant and was able to maintain her balance through a walk, trot, and canter. She could tell that George was pleased with her progress.

After her third day of lessons, she dismounted onto legs that felt like jelly, and she grabbed Clover's mane to steady herself. Clover playfully nudged her shoulder, pushing her toward the house, as if to say: We are done for the day. Go rest. You did well, my lady, and so did I. Now, where are the oats? George led Clover to the barn. Tomorrow he would help Miriam learn everything she would need to know in order to give her new horse all the love and care she deserved. Caroline, Elnora, and Cora laughed and clapped their hands in delight as Miriam hobbled gingerly across the barnyard to the house with a wide smile on her face. Caroline had drawn a bath for the girls in the big copper tub on the back porch. Miriam was encouraged to use it first to soak her aches and pains away. That night, her dreams were of horses, and she was in love.

Chapter 9 1883

The days flew by as Miriam helped Caroline and the girls design, create, and gather items for Elnora's trousseau. The family eagerly looked forward to the house-raising. George had given the young couple eighty fertile acres of his farm, and the stone foundation was already laid for a little frame house. Saturday was the day they would begin. After all the men had done their morning chores, neighbors, family, and church friends from far and wide would assemble at the new house site and begin work. Music and dancing would follow in the evening, and they would all spend the night sleeping under the stars, in lean-tos made of canvas, or in their covered wagons. The minister would call on Sunday morning for a short service, and, full of hotcakes and his blessing, they would add the finishing touches. Everyone from the groom's Methodist Episcopal Church would be there, and many hands made light work. As soon as the engagement was announced a year ago, the timber had all been hauled in from the woods and milled on the spot. It had been stickered and left to dry all summer in anticipation of the special day. Kegs of nails and roofing shingles were purchased from Churubusco and waited on the site. Every man would bring his own hand tools, and the boys would provide the muscle. The interior woodwork would be burled walnut, and the kitchen would feature cherry cabinets that would take on a rich red patina as the years went by. The flooring was going to be wide oak boards that would mellow to a lovely yellow-orange. This was going to be a beautiful little home: simple, airy, and efficient.

The girls bathed and selected their clothing with care. They helped each other with braids, hair ribbons, sashes, and dozens of buttons. Cora struggled with the buttonhook, so Miriam knelt and helped with her high boots and the tiny rounded buttons. Miriam was preoccupied with thoughts of Clover, but she made an effort to be cheerful and to turn her thoughts toward being social. She would be meeting lots of families from different sections of Smith and Thorncreek townships. George and his family had been so kind to her. She would never forget how they had helped her move on past her father's death. George was trying so hard to stand in for Pa, and, once in a while, her heart would skip a beat when a familiar profile was lighted by the flickering firelight. Several times since the funeral, Pa had appeared to Miriam in her dreams. He looked young and happy, and he smiled right at her. Her faith assured her he was blissful in the Great Beyond. She sensed he had found Willie and joyfully carried him on his shoulders through the golden streets of Heaven just as he had on the dusty streets of Churubusco. The thought gave her much comfort.

Ladies were unpacking their baskets when they arrived. All the foods of the season were shown off at their finest, and Miriam's mouth watered at the sight. She had not been eating well since Pa's death, and her party dress was about two sizes too big when the girls buttoned her up. They teased her about her prominent ribs and said she was getting so skinny she was about to disappear. The fresh air, sunshine, and the murmuring of a happy, excited crowd all served to whet her appetite. She recognized Tildy's famous cream pie and fried chicken on the groaning board and waved to Ma and Tildy, who were scurrying around visiting and laughing. This event was going to be Ma's first time out to socialize since Pa's death. It was so good for all of William's sons to join hands to build a house. This was just what the doctor ordered to bring them together after the tragedies of late. Selfish Tobias wouldn't allow Sis to come to the party, but even that wasn't going to put a damper on Miriam's good mood.

As she watched the men already straining to raise the walls, she recognized the boy who had spoken to her in the henhouse. What an odd place to make someone's acquaintance—she had to smile at that. She wondered if the "chicken coop" boy would remember her. At that moment, she was whirled out of her reverie by a giggling group of girls, and Cora introduced her to several pretty young women. They attended a different school and went to the little Methodist Episcopal Church on the banks of the Blue River.

The whole house was framed and sided before dusk. Left to do on Sunday would be the roofing and chimney-building. The heavy work was all completed in record time. The finishing touches of built-in cabinetry would be a contribution by James, Evan, and Frank as their wedding present to the couple. Sis, Ma, and Miriam were going to give hand-stitched curtains and bedding.

Men brought out a dozen torches fueled by coal oil and jabbed them into the ground around the perimeter of the house. Joseph Smith, a part time preacher, stood in the flickering flame with arms raised in supplication and led everyone in prayer.

Then three men tuned their fiddles and guitar and began to play "My Wild Irish Rose" and "Turkey in the Straw" while everyone else dug into the food. Fried chicken, ham, and a whole roast pig with an apple in its mouth graced the table. The hungry crowd dined on loaves of yeasty white bread, steamed brown bread, corn dodgers, potatoes, pickled eggs, beets, and cucumber pickles. Neighbors with ferocious appetites loaded plates with Paradise pudding with nutmeg and apples served with sweet sauce, tapioca, huckleberry pudding, mincemeat pie with chopped beef tongue and currents, fruit turnovers, jelly cakes, gingersnaps, and Sally Lunn cake. It was a veritable feast for the eyes and the stomach and God's blessing on the fine men, women, and children of the land.

Miriam and several other girls settled at the base of one of the two maple trees that would be beautiful orange landmarks framing the dooryard each fall. The torchlight illuminated all the faces around her as neighbors reveled in this opportunity to get together. Several men rode off on horseback to do their evening feeding and milking, but they waved their hats and whooped as they galloped away, assuring everyone they would be back in the "shake of a lamb's tail."

The hard cider keg was tapped, and

many of the men and boys stood with mugs waiting. Deep laughter emanated from that shadowy corner of the yard. Miriam felt the presence of someone standing in the shadows to her right. To her surprise, she glanced up and into the smiling face of the "chicken coop" boy. He appeared to have grown a foot since she had last seen him. He wore store-bought denim pants held up by black suspenders. The sleeves of his light gray shirt were rolled up to his elbows. His hair was parted in the middle and still wet and shiny from joining the other men at the well to wash up for dinner.

He introduced himself to her this time. David M. Pence—everybody just called him Dave. She told him her name, and he shyly responded that he knew her name already. He had asked Evan when he saw him in town but made Evan promise not to tell her he had asked. He looked down at her with a sheepish grin. He was juggling a big plate of food, and he suddenly sat down by her, uninvited. Her friends giggled and excused themselves. They abandoned her. She had never been by herself in the dark with a boy before, but he was so relaxed and so obviously famished from the day's hard work, she had to laugh at the way he attacked his food. He tucked into a large piece of freshly buttered and salted corn on the cob—and the juice squirted out onto her skirt. He produced a sawdust-covered handkerchief out of a back pocket and began to awkwardly rub her skirt. She reached out and put her hand on his wrist to stop him from unintentionally making a bad thing so much worse. He froze at her touch, and her hand stayed just two heartbeats longer than she had intended—but they both felt those heartbeats—and the ice was broken between them. They set their plates aside and settled back against the tree to visit. He was not shy once he began to talk, and the words just seemed to pour out of Miriam. They had so much in common—two young lives both spent on farms in Smith Township. He was just one year older and had finished his common school education last year. He had graduated with honors and he loved to read. There sparked an instant friendship and understanding between them, and the quiet laughter from under the maple caused some giggles from her friends, who were secretly watching.

Pa had taught her the basic square dancing steps, and, as fiddle music filled the air, the calls began. Dave jumped up and extended his hand toward Miriam. He lifted her from the base of the tree as if she were as light as a feather. He smiled down on her. Goodness, he *had* grown a foot! She gaily waved to Ma and Tildy. Tildy looked as if she could be knocked over by a feather as she watched Miriam go by hand-in-hand with a tall dark-headed young man. As she turned to comment to the missus, Tildy saw her hurrying over to a gathering of women, who looked with interest and then turned back to tell her what they knew about this boy. Tildy watched the missus step back, nod, and smile.

The animated neighbors stomped and whirled to the caller's instructions. The men swung their partners round and round, going through the complicated, fluid motions of the square dance. The open living area made a wonderful dance floor: thumps of boots on planking, long dresses swishing, smiles flashing, and fiddle music sending strident sounds aloft on the warm light breeze. The caller rhythmically stomped his foot, clapped his hands, and called out to the dancers in a strong melodic voice.

The owls and other night creatures had their hunting interrupted by this unexpected frolic of the humans, who were normally counted upon to withdraw quietly into their houses shortly after dusk. Only the bats were delighted; they swooped and wheeled to catch the moths attracted by the light, and when Miriam and Dave took a break, breathless from the last dance and the newness of their acquaintance, a large, delicate luna moth glided in, landed, and settled on Dave's lapel—a living boutonniere. He stood stock-still while they admired its pale green wings and oval antennae. Miriam had never seen one of these creatures so closely before and couldn't resist gently touching one of the wings. A light fairy dust of white scales glowed on her index finger—not enough to mar the moth's spectacular beauty—but just enough to remind the young couple how life was precious and fragile. After a time, slowly, burdened by its beautiful but cumbersome wings, the moth climbed haltingly to Dave's shoulder. As they watched, holding their breath, its perfectly designed wings caught the evening breeze. The luminous insect rose slowly and gracefully into the flickering light. It glided in one unhurried circle around their heads and was gone: up, up, ethereal into the night sky.

It was a magical moment, bringing the young couple together in a way that music and dancing could not equal. They stood in silence for a long time, hearts beating; no words could do honor to what they had just witnessed. It was late. Families were moving toward their sleeping quarters. Dave took both of her hands in his, looked into her eyes, smiled wistfully, and walked away. Miriam's feet never touched the ground as she joined George's family to drive back to his house for the night in order to help bring back Sunday breakfast. She seemed to be moving in slow motion, senses muffled, and she was asleep almost before her head hit the pillow.

Chapter 10 1883

When Miriam returned to her home place, she glided in triumphantly on Clover. Ma was surprised to see her daughter ride up the lane on an elegant horse, sitting ramrod straight, ladylike, and dignified in the saddle. So that was what George was up to. One look at Miriam's face told her all she needed to know. Happiness, contentment, and excitement shone forth, and it warmed her heart. Evan was green with envy. He didn't have such a fine riding horse, but he was the owner of a buggy that was the newest and best model. He had used some money his father had put aside for him—in fact, he used all the money put aside—but he knew he started some hearts fluttering when he asked the girls to go riding with him.

Miriam was bursting with excitement as she ran Clover through her paces for her mother. Ma had never ridden a saddle horse and marveled at the clever way the side-saddle was constructed. She told Miriam she would begin right away to make her a dark green riding habit like one she had seen in town. It would have a split skirt covered for modesty by a full apron. In the back of Ma's mind, however, was a little resentment toward George. It seemed like he should have asked her permission before making it possible for Miriam to ride out by herself. Somehow it didn't seem quite seemly or safe for a young woman to be encouraged to ride the roads without a chaperone. Liz had always ridden in the company of her husband, and now her son. What would a potential suitor think to see Miriam riding along as high and mighty as you please on such a beautiful horse? Would she be putting on airs? Ma watched her daughter ride round and round with such a smile on her face. Could she deny her this happiness? Perhaps it was happiness she, herself, had missed with the constant pregnancies and responsibilities of her youth. Perhaps Miriam would be a more modern woman, for better or for worse.

Ma thought about the tender way Dave Pence treated Miriam at the house-raising. On Sunday afternoon, she looked around for them and discovered they had stolen away together to walk down by the Blue River. Ma felt guilty spying, but she glimpsed them together on the river bank and smiled to see her daughter's new beau showing Miriam how to skip stones on the water. Dave showed off to beat the band, and Miriam gazed upon him with admiration. Liz thought back to her own courtship and marriage. William had been so much older than she, but he exuded such confidence, sense of adventure, and desire to get ahead that she was attracted to him immediately. He knew his own mind, and it was obvious immediately after their meeting, he dreamed about her being an important part of his plans. At first, her father refused to give William her hand, but William was a man of action, and his persistence and charm won the dear old man over, too. William's father, John, came back to Ohio with the news of homesteading opportunities in newly opened Indiana, land that had been clearly surveyed and marked off in square, indisputable sections. John's memories of living in squalor in Ireland with no land for the common man and no chance to leave a legacy to one's children spurred him to decisively count out $1,200 cash onto the land office counter in Fort Wayne on behalf of his son. Miriam and William hired Tildy to help, packed their wagon, and left both their families behind. Liz was barely out of her teens, with a two year old on her lap and with another child on the way, as they rattled away northwest to the section of land John had reserved for them.

Miriam looked over her shoulder as she swept by on Clover and saw her mother looking troubled. She had never considered that Ma might not approve of her learning to ride. She would die if she had to return Clover to George. "Please, Ma. Please, Ma," she whispered. Clover sensed that the joy had gone out of her rider. She slowed to a walk and came right over to the tired looking woman. Without any urging, Clover looked at Ma with understanding, gentle eyes and brought her nose forward to be patted. It was Clover's greeting, and it had made many an instant friend in the past. A slow smile spread over Ma's face, as the horse stood patiently to be recognized, and Ma reached out and stroked her nose and patted her broad neck. Miriam dismounted and gave her mother the warmest, most intimate, hug of their lives. Their eyes misted for a moment before Ma brightened and said, "Well, you had better put that pretty animal of yours in the barn and hurry in to dinner. We have an awful lot to do before you ride to the church on Sunday to give your testimonial." Miriam and Clover, thankful to have passed a most important test, headed toward Clover's new stall—and home—in the barn.

Miriam was scheduled to join the Merriam Christian Chapel on Sunday, and Ma was very excited for her. Now that she was done with school, her acceptance of Christ as her Savior would mark the rite of passage from girl to young woman. She would always remember Miriam's smile when she put Miriam's Grandfather John Coulter's New Testament in her hands—the book he carried on the ship from Ireland in 1809 to begin the Coulter family's adventure in the New World. William had asked Liz to give it to Miriam prior to her joining the church. Miriam planned to hold this New Testament as she spoke her testimony in church. Inside the stained brown leather cover, William's father had written:

"John Coulter is my name,
And Ireland is my station.
Petigo is my native place,
And Christ is my salvation.
Remember thy Covenant and break it not.
Lest in the day thou do it
By God you may be to judgment brought.
As He is judge high over all.
He looks and sees both great and small.
John Coulter, Sunday, 3rd November, 1803."

All week, Ma and Tildy rehearsed the Christian Chapel creed with Miriam. She would be asked to recite the beliefs held in common by all who joined the little brick church. She would also be asked to give her personal testimonial of faith. This was serious business because she had always been taught to be good for her word. Pa said your word is as good as your bond. That meant when you promised something, you followed through. When you borrowed something, you returned it in the same or better condition. When you made a pledge or swore an oath, you gave your life to uphold it, if need be. There were absolutely no exceptions to this hard and fast rule. So, if she stood in front of God and the congregation of neighbors, family, and friends and told them she believed in the same things they had pledged to, she was committed to the church and those in it forever. End of story. Just as she would say "I do" someday to a man, there would never be an "I don't." Ma said it was something called integrity; it was one of the three most important qualities a man or woman could have in this life: integrity, the love of God, and respect for His power.

On Sunday, in the hearing of all present and in the heavenly presence of God and her Pa, Miriam stood, turned to face the congregation, took a deep breath, and recited the creed:

"I believe in one Triune God, eternally existing in three persons – Father, Son, and Holy Spirit, co-eternal in being, co-identical in nature, co-equal in power and glory and having the same attributes and perfections. I believe in the Holy Scriptures of the Old and New Testaments to be the verbally inspired Word of God, wholly inerrant in the original writing, infallible and God-breathed, the final authority for faith and life. I believe that the Lord Jesus Christ, the eternal Son of God, became man, without ceasing to be God, having been conceived by the Holy Spirit and born of the Virgin Mary, in order that He might reveal God and redeem sinful men. I believe that the Lord Jesus Christ accomplished our redemption through His death on the cross as a representative, substitutionary sacrifice in providing an unlimited atonement for the sins of the whole world; and that our justification is made sure by His literal, physical resurrection from the dead. I believe that the Lord Jesus Christ ascended to heaven and is now exalted at the right hand of God where, as your High Priest, He fulfills the ministry of Representative, Intercessor, and Advocate. "

Miriam continued to recite her beliefs in salvation as the gift of God, through belief in Jesus Christ's sacrifice on the cross. She recited the assurance that once saved and born again, she would be secure in Christ's love for her lifetime. She recited her belief in the rites of baptism and Holy Communion, and her belief in the body of the church and its mission to reach out to all mankind. She stated her belief in the literal, bodily, personal second coming of Christ as a blessed hope for those, like herself, who had accepted Christ as their savior. Before she took her seat, Miriam looked around at those seated in front of her and at the minister. She thanked each and every one of them for their support of her and her family in both good and bad times. She thanked God for her family and for her wonderful father who rested in peace in the cemetery next door. She pledged to support the church and the members of the congregation in any way she could and trusted that God would lead her to be of service in the community her whole life through. She turned to the older people, who gathered in the front pews in order to better hear the service, and thanked them for following God's leading to a great place on earth and for their abiding faith and strength. She spoke to the children, who were earnestly listening, and reminded them of their charge to honor their fathers and mothers and to do good works—that God gives spiritual gifts to all believers, big and small.

Miriam sat down beside her mother. Her face was flushed with emotion. Her affirmation of faith had been a much more powerful experience than she had expected. She felt as if, all of a sudden, she had become a woman. It was overwhelming to sense that God Himself had heard her words, and her heart felt light, as if a stone had been rolled away.

CHAPTER 11 1883

After their midday meal following her testimony, Miriam tried to sew with drooping eyelids. At one point, she poked herself with her needle, and Ma finally laughed and suggested Miriam go up to her room to take a nap. She awoke to the sound of conversation in the parlor below and went to the window to see who had come to call. A light covered buggy pulled by a sleek brown horse with a fancy harness was tied to the post in the drive. Evan and Frank were walking around and around the buggy admiring the silver studs on the bridle and the glossy black finish on the wheels. They saw her in the window and started to make faces at her, pointing excitedly to the parlor window. What a couple of silly boys. Her mother suddenly knocked at her bedroom door and explained that a Mr. Pence had come to call on her. Ma smiled and asked Miriam if she was accepting callers. She chuckled as Miriam's eyes widened and she turned for her mirror and hairbrush. Ma helped her find a pretty wool dress, for, Ma explained, Dave had asked her permission to take her out for a little drive, and she would need something warmer. Ma brought her own shawl for Miriam to put over her shoulders and went on downstairs to tell Dave to be patient a few more minutes. Miriam looked at herself in the mirror. This was the second time today she had felt her face flush, and this time she could see her cheeks redden in the mirror. What would he think? She was acting as silly as some of the flighty girls at school. Oh, well, he would just have to take her the way she was, no getting around it, but she was having a day with so many powerful feelings, she felt on the verge of tears. Good heavens.

Dave stood as she entered the parlor. His hat dangled from his long fingers as he nervously fussed with the brim. He was really suffering under the scrutiny of her mother, brothers, and Tildy. A bead of sweat ran down from his hairline to the back of his collar, but, now that he saw Miriam, everyone else seemed to fade away. When she shyly smiled at him, he was transported. The couple, glad to be getting out of the public eye, walked quickly to the buggy. Dave offered Miriam his arm, and he helped her into the seat. She ran her hands over the leather upholstery and admired the small brown buggy horse that was stamping in impatience, too. Clover peered from the paddock, ears on alert, and wondered what stranger was taking her lady away.

Dave steered the buggy in a sweeping turn in the barnyard and then headed down the lane—the horse's hooves clip-clopping right along. Miriam was glad she had a shawl and pulled it over her shoulders. They soon fell back into their easy way of chatting. Miriam liked the way she could always be genuine around Dave, and she suspected he was glad to not have to put on any artificiality to impress her.

Dave and Miriam began a regular pattern of courtship. After his Methodist church service was over, he drove the buggy to the Coulter's farm and waited for Miriam to get ready to take a ride. When the weather got too chilly, he would put his horse in the barn and come in to have Sunday dinner with the family and to spend the afternoon. He had learned to bring a pocketful of corn kernels to ward off the peacock attacks. Dave liked to tease Ma and hear her laugh, and she blushed and made a fuss over him. Miriam even told the family about her silly nickname for Dave—her "chicken coop" boy. The Pences would often send a cake or bag of hickory nuts along with Dave for his contribution Sunday supper, and he and Miriam would spend time around the fireplace crushing the hickory nuts and picking out the strong-flavored meats. Dave got along well with James and Frank, too. They spent time in the barn looking at the livestock, and, once in a while, the boys treated Dave to a nip from the bottle they kept out of sight of their Ma. Tildy liked to see him come through the back door on Sundays, shucking off his warm woolen coat, and she always had a hug and a cup of hot coffee ready for him. Ma finally took down Pa's old jacket from the hook to make room for Dave's coat and hat, an action not unnoticed by the family.

Miriam was looking forward to her first visit to the large brick home on the Pence farm. Dave invited her to come to celebrate his father's birthday on the 20th of November. She would meet the whole family for the first time, and she was plenty nervous since she would be staying overnight in Dave's imposing house.

Dave acted as excited as a puppy when he arrived on the Coulter farm to get her. He had a new buffalo robe waiting to cover her lap and gave her his arm as they slipped and slid across the icy barnyard. The horse snorted a cloud of vapor and stamped its feet in the cold. Dave tossed her carpetbag in the back of the buggy, waved to Ma and Tildy, and off they went. The air was biting and Miriam snuggled close to Dave. They had shared their first awkward kiss under an orange harvest moon several weeks before, and she was feeling very sure of her place in his life. In fact, she was beginning to think she could not face life without his friendship and affection. Was this love? Well, if it wasn't, she didn't know what it was. A gamey odor arose from the heavy robe, but it felt wonderfully warm, and the coarse, curly hair caught the snowflakes—their brilliant facets glistening as the sun peeked intermittently from behind the dark snow clouds.

Miriam asked Dave to tell her a little about whom she would be meeting in order to quell her nerves. She would be introduced to the whole family today, even Uncle Judd, who was down from his job on the railroad in Gary. Judd, the youngest of the siblings, was the only one of the Pence boys who didn't want to be a farmer, and he loved to come home and tell stories of his life in the big city outside of Chicago and of his train travels. She would meet Dave's younger sister, Florence, who was the scholar in the family—quite the bookworm. Miriam would be sleeping on the daybed in Florence's room, and, if she could pry Florence's nose out of her book, Dave assured her they would become friends. Miriam made a mental note to be especially nice to her. She would meet his older brother Jim and his new wife, Alice. Dave liked to tease Jim about his lengthy moniker: James Abraham Lincoln Pence, and he had always reveled in shouting Jim's whole name to call him to dinner. Jim was doing a great job farming his own place now, and they had their first baby girl named Ollie. Even though Jim was only two years his elder, Dave said Jim was not letting the grass grow under his feet, and he admired him. He and Jim had enjoyed growing up together, had shared many experiences, and Dave hoped they could always stay close friends and companions. His oldest sister, Mary, would be at the gathering. She was a strong and determined woman and reminded him the most of Miriam's mother. She was a wonderful seamstress, and her two youngsters, Minnie and Jess, were good children. She was married to Joseph Smith, who was a part-time farmer and preacher, and he could be counted on to ask a lengthy blessing before each meal. Miriam shouldn't take a bite until Joseph had his say, no matter how much her stomach rumbled, he added with a wink.

They arrived before Dave had a chance to tell Miriam anything about his mother and father, but she felt more confident negotiating the lay of the land at the Pence household. She saw the imposing two story house as soon as they came around a sharp curve. Its mellow dark bricks were set off by white columns on the front porch. Two walk-out windows onto the porch roof allowed access to a cool sleeping area in the summer. The house sat elevated on the south side of the road, with a huge barn opposite. The Blue River sparkled in its icy course just beyond the house, and a grove of large white pines in front of the house were blanketed with the freshly fallen snow. The snow was pelting down out of an ominous sky, and the buggy wheels slid a bit as they turned into the short drive.

A blast of warm air hit Miriam as Dave ushered her through the back door into the kitchen. A kindly woman looked up through the aromatic vapors rising from the pots and pans on the massive cook stove. She wiped her hands on her apron and greeted Miriam. She took Miriam's wraps and scolded Dave for bringing his girl in through the back door instead of escorting her onto their front porch and making some sort of a grand entrance. Dave smiled and looked sheepish. Miriam understood. Tildy would have scolded her, too. Women hated having guests walk through their kitchens upon arrival. What else were fancy front doors for? The fragrance of baking bread assailed her, and she glanced to see the cook hurry over and remove four crispy loaves from a brick oven built into the chimney stack.

The family, obviously stationed at the front door to greet them, came streaming back to the pantry to lead Miriam into the house proper. Florence greeted Miriam with a gracious smile and told her she was glad her big brother had found such a lovely friend. Florence reminded Dave to bring in Miriam's bag. In his excitement, he had left it in the buggy. Jim got him off the hook by offering to take care of his rig while he introduced Miriam to everyone. Miriam and Dave found themselves ushered through the hallway and finally seated next to one another on the horsehair divan in the parlor. Dave's siblings all looked kindly upon the couple with a sense of relief. Each one of them had been wondering if Dave could conquer his shy ways and speak up to a girl. The brothers and sisters could tell from the awkward blush on the couple's faces that they all needed to stop staring and to settle into normal Pence behavior before Miriam fled in terror, so they found places to sit, and the children went back to their puzzle games on the parlor floor. Miriam had her first chance to look around. They were seated in a beautiful room with high ceilings and warm woodwork. The walls were plastered and a few pictures hung around the room. She was glad to see a portrait of Jesus prominently displayed with its accompanying Bible verse. The comforting and familiar picture reminded her to breathe, and she was trying to think of something to contribute to the quiet conversation, when suddenly the children sprang from the floor and stood stock-still. All the adults rose, as well, and Dave put his hand under Miriam's elbow so she could stand beside him. What in the world was happening?

Into the room strode a tall, bearded man in a well-cut, dark suit under a black wool coat ornamented with gleaming silver buttons. He carried a shiny beaver top hat in his hand. He looked around the room, making an appraisal of each person, and silence reigned. His eyes finally found Miriam, and he took three long strides to stand in front of her She raised her head to look into his eyes. He nodded to Dave, awaiting an introduction, and Dave formally said, "Father, I would like you to meet our friend and neighbor Miriam Coulter. Miriam, this is my father, Joseph J. Pence." The imposing man's face softened a bit as he held her gaze. Yes, she looked like her pa—a man he had admired very much for his strength and integrity. William Coulter had been one of the county's best men. This girl came from good stock, had a steady light in her eyes, and looked him straight on. None of the others had been able to do that. JJ was known for making quick, accurate judgments about both people and acreage, and he liked this gal. This Miriam had spirit—the Irish in her, no doubt. His quiet son had done well.

A hint of a smile appeared through his grizzled beard, and Miriam knew she had passed some sort of very important test from this harsh man of sober German ancestry. He formally welcomed her to his home, nodded to the couple to encourage them to take their seats, and the whole family visibly relaxed. Mary took her father's coat and the cook came with some soft woolen slippers for his feet. He sat with a sigh onto what had to be his chair, a cushioned oak rocker. He noted the grandchildren playing contentedly on the floor near his feet, lifted little Ollie onto his lap, perused the farm market column in the *Commercial Mail*, and basked in the presence of his family on his birthday. It was apparent to Miriam the family revolved around this impressive man, as the planets around the sun. He was so different from Pa. She felt sort of sorry for Dave having had to grow up under this man's imperious thumb.

Mary called everyone to the table, and Miriam was seated next to Dave and to the right of Mr. Pence as befitting her place as honored guest. She thought it strange that the woman who cooked for them took a place at the foot of the table, but it was closest to the kitchen, so, if she, like Tildy, was in the habit of eating with the family, that would be the logical place for her. As Miriam looked around the table, she realized that she had not met Dave's mother and wondered about her absence. As she recollected, Dave had never really said anything about his mother. He said that Mary took a very active place in running the household, and that was apparent. After a prolonged grace was offered by Joseph, as Dave had predicted, everyone began passing the dishes of sliced roast beef, mashed potatoes, glazed carrots that had been brought up crisp from the root cellar through the trapdoor in the kitchen floor, and warm slices of crusty bread served with freshly churned pats of butter molded into the shape of little pineapples. My, oh, my, everything was wonderful; this family took eating seriously. Miriam politely asked the cook if she could please bring some salt to the table, but, instead, Mary looked startled, rustled off to the kitchen, and placed a tiny crystal salt dish and spoon at Miriam's place. Looks were exchanged around the table, and Miriam uneasily began to think the joke, whatever it was, might be on her. Later, when she spilled a little gravy on her dress, she asked the hired help if she could please bring her a damp towel to blot it. Again, Mary jumped up to tend to her. This time, however, the stern lady at the foot of the table asked Miriam if she knew who she was. Miriam's face flushed and she turned to Dave for help. He whispered, "This is Alice. She is my stepmother who raised me since I was seven."

Miriam's eyes flashed at him in anger and embarrassment. She turned to the family and asked them to beg her forgiveness. She had not been adequately introduced all around, and she feared she had caused offense. "Mrs. Pence, I am sorry for my forward behavior. I hope you will forgive me my ignorance." She asked to be excused because she wasn't feeling well, pushed her own chair away from the table, and strode up the staircase before Dave could even extricate his long legs from his chair.

She shut the door to the bedroom behind her and the tears began to fall. She had made such a terrible impression—but these people were so quiet and sullen. If the tables had been turned, Pa would have given Dave a hearty welcome: a slap on the back and perhaps a small glass of whiskey to seal their friendship and connection, instead of staging a staring contest from on high. These nervous and sober people tiptoed around their father. Imagine, she thought Mrs. Pence was the hired woman. How could Dave have put her in that position? Oh, she was mad!

She looked out the window. It was long past dusk and continuing to snow. She was stuck here in this untenable position. Well, maybe not. She had begun to pack her things in order to go down and ask Dave to transport her home in their sleigh, when a light knock was heard at the door. Florence peeked in and asked to be admitted. Miriam turned her back so she could not see her tears and heard Florence's skirts rustle as she sat down on her rope bed across the room. When Florence spoke to Miriam, her voice broke, and Miriam turned to see tears of empathy welling in Florence's eyes, too. Before Miriam knew it, she and Florence were in each other's arms, all emotions pouring out and the anxiety of the evening melting away. Florence said she understood Miriam's anger at her stupid brother for being so backward and excited that he didn't make sure she was safe and comfortable in their home. She said she watched her father put her through the eye contact test that he used to judge all his children's intended husbands and wives, and that Miriam had been the first one to pass with flying colors. She told Miriam that the whole family had rained down on Dave's head after she left the table, telling him what a fool he would be to let someone as wonderful as you slip through his fingers. He had left the table as if he were being stoned and had fled to the barn. Florence begged with Miriam to stay the night with her to become friends. She encouraged Miriam to confront Dave and to help him understand how his thoughtlessness had embarrassed and hurt her deeply, to talk privately with Mary and Alice in order for them to assure her no harm had been done, and to shake her father's hand in mutual respect before they went to their evening's rest. Could she do it? Yes, Miriam thought she could, but she had to talk to Dave first. The outcome of this dreadful evening all rested on his shoulders.

Florence helped Miriam bundle up in her coat, scarf, boots, hat and gloves, and pointed out the direction of the barn through the darkness and falling snow. Miriam could see a lantern burning in one of the windows, so she leaned into the wind and picked her way across the slippery county road. When she lifted the latch and pulled open the door, Dave stood up, stricken, from a stool in the workshop, and she could see grief in his eyes. In three strides, she was in his arms and her face was pressed into his shoulder. She could feel his shoulders shake as he sobbed. "Oh, I am so afraid you will leave me, Miriam. I was so stupid to cast you into the lion's den. I had no idea the pressure I was putting you under by bringing you here today—and then to be so thoughtless. I would rather die than have you embarrassed in front of my family, but what can I do now? I have been sitting here trying to figure this out. I wouldn't blame you if you wanted me to hitch up the sleigh and take you home, but I cannot imagine a day without seeing you, a day without your friendship. Can you *ever* forgive me?"

Miriam took a big breath, summoned her strength, and pushed Dave out to arm's length. He was as weak as a kitten. She led him to the stool and bade him sit down. She stood right in front of him, held both his hands gently, and looked him straight in the eyes. "Dave, you know I'm awfully mad—more disappointed than mad, I guess. This evening has made me realize I need to tell you what sort of woman you will get if you pledge your troth to me, so I just want you to listen while I say my piece. This won't take long. Afterward, you can decide whether to hitch the sleigh or not.

"I am young. I am small of stature,

but I'm not a child or a possession. I left childhood things behind in the last few years when I buried my brother then and my father. God consecrated a grown woman on the day I gave my affirmation of faith to the church. On that day, I vowed to be of service to my community—not just to my family, but to a much larger circle—and I am committed to having my mother teach me everything she knows about the healing arts. I am strong physically and emotionally. I am a capable horsewoman and have ridden these roads and fields without the help or accompaniment of a man, and I intend to continue riding and reaching out in Christian love to area neighbors, friends, and maybe even foes, whether I marry or not. I feel that is my calling. My dearest friend, this is the hardest thing I have ever had to say, but if you desire a partner who will be a cook, housekeeper, mother of eleven, clothes washer, and quilt maker—in other words, if you want a woman who will be like my mother and Tildy combined for your wife— you do not want me, for I am to be none of these for you."

Miriam looked deeply into Dave's eyes. She was dry-eyed and her voice was gentle, but strong. She had told him everything in her heart, except that she loved him, and, without him, she doubted if there would ever be anyone else. This was neither the time for tears nor for a profession of love. She had cast her dice, and the risks were so great she was nearly overwhelmed. She stepped back, slowed her anxious breathing, and quietly waited.

Dave was silent after he listened to her sincere words, and he thought about all she had both said and implied. This evening had been a disaster, but, he could see clearly, it was a necessary trial, and the stresses on both of them were revealing life's realities unclouded by passion. He had presumed she would become a woman like her mother. Why would she want to be anything different? Her mother was wonderful. He carried a shadowy remembrance of his real mother, Susan. She had worked by his father's side to tame the wilderness, and he and she had labored over the building of the big house together. They had mined the sticky clay from the creek bank, molded it into bricks, and fired them in a homemade kiln. Together, they laid brick upon brick—a fifteen year project of massive scale. His mother died an untimely death at thirty-two, only one short year after the house was finished. Dave's grandparents railed against his father for working their daughter to death and compelling her to have baby after baby, six children beginning when she was but herself a child of eighteen. There remained resentment between the Waughs and his father to this day. But if Miriam was not going to provide the kind of partnership he needed to continue the Pence farming tradition, three generations of success in Whitley County, what would that mean for his life? He knew some men who married, moved to town, and abandoned their claim on the soil. Could she possibly be suggesting that? Father had promised him some land, and he had envisioned the frame farmhouse he was planning to build, the Angus cattle that would populate his pastures, and his children running rosy-cheeked in the yard. An evening spoiled—but a life spoiled, too?

The only sounds in the barn were the sputter of the lantern and the large workhorses shifting in their stalls. There really wasn't anything more to say. After some agonizing moments, Dave stood, pulled the harness from the hook, and slowly walked toward the horse that would transport them to Miriam's home. She understood he had made a monumental decision, so she left the barn, turned her face into the blowing snow, and waded toward the house to collect her things. She was chilled to the bone. If this break up had to happen, she wanted to get this over quickly and get home to Ma. The bells on the sleigh harness jingled cruelly as the dry-eyed and somber couple rode in silence through the snowy night, and Miriam could only wonder what the Pences were thinking as they heard the sleigh turn onto the dark county road and the sounds fade away into the distance.

Chapter 12 1883

A subdued Thanksgiving passed, and the snow blew into deep drifts in the barnyard during the first two weeks of December. Ma and Miriam stayed snug by the fire while Evan spent most of his days outdoors performing the minimal winter chores and trapping muskrat and mink along the river. The two women began to pore over the *Memorial Edition of Dr. Chase's Receipt Book and Household Physician* Ma had bought for Miriam's graduation present. Dr. Chase had sold over a million copies of this thick tome that pledged to convey "Practical Knowledge for the People." After Willie's death, they were determined to learn everything possible about the diseases of women and children. Ma's childbearing days were long gone, but she wanted to arm Miriam with the most up-to-date information on medicine, and Dr. Chase's book would be a good start in this isolated country. The small town doctor who made house calls and attended Willie's sickbed was getting old, and Ma was convinced he hadn't kept up with the latest in modern treatments.

Ma worried about Miriam, who hadn't been forthcoming during the last month about her sudden break with Dave.

When asked, Miriam just said she had realized they could not get along as well as she had hoped, and Ma figured she would tell her more when she was ready. Ma and the boys missed Dave's presence on Sundays. The house seemed very quiet without his laughter and tenderness. Ma had watched Miriam look wistfully at the empty coat hook by the back door. In order to mend Miriam's heartbreak, Ma offered to pay for nursing school and told her she would even do her best to help pay for Miriam's training to become a doctor. At first, Miriam scoffed at the idea, but Ma could see, as their studies continued, Miriam was beginning to seriously consider the offer. It would be highly unusual, but not impossible, for a woman to become a physician, if she was willing to go East for her education. Ma suggested Miriam could find a medical school in the Cincinnati area, where she had Jenkins aunts and uncles to furnish room and board. If she could not get training to become a doctor, at least she could come back as a qualified nurse and a trained midwife, a position in short supply in the rural areas.

Among the many maladies in Dr. Chase's book, Miriam and Ma studied: treating croup with hot onion poultices to the chest; curing headaches with compresses of spirits of hartshorn and camphor; and the many current and varied remedies for consumption, also called tuberculosis. They concocted cough syrups from Ma's store of dried herbs and roots. The doctor recommended: "horehound leaves and blossoms, spikenard root, comfrey root, elecampane root, and sunflower seeds, one ounce each boiled and strained and mixed with brandy." They studied how to treat the sting and danger of frostbite, rid the body of tape worms, and sooth swollen tonsils by blowing baking soda through a paper straw onto them. They were particularly interested in the cannabis sativa remedy for the treatment of bronchitis, asthma, catarrh, and nervous complaints promoted by Dr. Stevens' East India Consumption Cure. Almost all of the medicines could be gathered from their land, from along the ditches, or from their garden. Both women were eagerly looking forward to the return of the gathering season next spring.

Miriam was feeling desperate to cultivate a new passion. She remembered a fall long ago when she thought life was sweeter than ever. The harvest was one of the best, and Pa looked happy as he read by the firelight. Ma was busy with her needle every evening and had been taking young Miriam to the woods and fields to introduce her to the medicinal plants and herbs. Ma had taught her respect for the Indian lore that used the power of nature to heal, and she had always kept a supply of dried herbs to make spring tonics, poultices, and broths for the sick. Miriam's favorite foray as a child was when she and her mother gathered wild peppermint from the ditch banks to dry for tea. The oil from the mint smelled sweet and fresh, and she went to sleep with the fragrance still on her hands. She desperately wished she could have the sweet, carefree peppermint dreams of childhood again.

Dr. Chase devoted forty pages of his book to the topic of women's health, menses, and childbirth. When Liz saw Miriam took a special interest in the best medical practices during pregnancy and childbirth, she was able to add much to what was in the book. Her life experience had made her an expert in these areas. Not only had she borne eleven babies, she had assisted in the births of many more. The women of the church had often found comfort in having Liz attend them during labor, and Tildy had always been willing to watch the children while William drove her to assist. William was always a jovial comfort to the nervous fathers, as well, and could keep them busy and out from underfoot as the women attended to their business of bringing new life into the world.

If there were pregnancy complications, sometimes the doctor would be called, but most of the time the delivery was accomplished without much muss and fuss—just lots of pain followed by prayers of thanksgiving and joy. A number of times in her experience, however, Liz found herself in the position to have to console a family because of the loss of a mother or child during childbirth. She was uniquely qualified to understand the depth of their feelings upon that sort of dreadful loss. She also had assisted in deliveries where she knew the child might not have a loving home but was considered merely another "mouth to feed." She would always make it a practice to ride out to make regular calls on those women and babies to lend encouragement and help. She worked behind the scenes to alert her minister to a family's struggles and always was gratified to later see the same family filling a pew— healthy, happy baby in arms and voices raised in song.

Ma decided, at the next opportunity, she would have Evan drive her and Miriam to show her childbirth firsthand. Miriam needed to know the whole range of human behavior—the good and the bad, the joy and the sorrow. Next spring, she and Miriam would take their new knowledge into the fields and forest for herbs, flowers, and roots to add to their arsenal of cures. People sometimes scoffed and called these cures "folk medicine," or "quack cures," but Elizabeth felt certain that by joining the old ways and the new—and utilizing a good dose of common sense—fevers like those that took two of her babies could be defeated.

CHAPTER 13 1883

The Coulters had received absolutely no word from the Pence household since Miriam's disastrous experience at their table. When Evan and Frank went to town for supplies, Dave was nowhere to be found. Either he was busy on the farm, or he was doing a good job of avoiding them. Miriam didn't go to town for fear of running into a Pence or someone who would be compelled to gossip about her in the general store. Those neighbors in her church were too thoughtful to fuss over her. They didn't know the Pence family well, anyway, but they loved their Miriam, and they had plenty of other boys in mind for this wonderful girl.

So, it was a shock when, a week before Christmas Day, Miriam heard familiar sleigh bells turning up the lane. She had been gathering the eggs, and she stopped abruptly and fled into the house, dashed past Ma and ran up the stairs to her room, leaving a stream of frigid outside air in her wake. Miriam took off her coat and boots. She was chilled, and so she hopped into bed and pulled the covers to her chin. She sat motionless and listened. What could he want, if that was, indeed, Dave approaching? Her cheeks were flushed with the cold and the lingering embarrassment, anger, and aching loss she felt every time Dave crossed her mind. There was still a hole in her heart that had not been filled with anything but sorrow. She dared not face him.

She heard a knock. Tildy answered. Gentle footfalls moved into the parlor beneath her room followed by muffled voices...back and forth...back and forth...a quiet conversation of not just one woman and one man, but two deep voices were heard in the parlor. Tildy was making tea. Miriam could hear the sounds of the best teacups coming out of the cupboard and the hiss of the kettle. She would not go down, even if her mother called to her. The next thing she knew, she heard the front door close, the whinny of a horse, and sleigh bells rang away down the lane. She must have dozed off while listening to the monotonous, mumbled voices from below. Whoever had come was leaving. She didn't even want to know, so she didn't approach the window.

A light knock and Ma entered. She had a tender look on her face, as she pulled a chair over to Miriam's bed and gently took her hands in her own. "Miriam, I have just had a remarkable conversation with two very good neighbors and have been asked to give you a message from an earnest young man and his father." Ma continued despite Miriam's rankling at the word father—his *father* came, too?   "Mr. Pence said he was not representing his son. Dave could speak for himself.   He was, instead, an emissary from his wife and children.   He began by explaining what happened on his birthday and expressed how sorry the family was that they got off to such a bad start in getting to know you.

"Dave was very contrite.   He said that he and his sister Florence talked late into the night about your words to him. He has been thinking day and night about what you said about the kind of wife you would not be.   He still does not know all your thoughts about love and marriage, but he has reached one decision.   He cannot let you out of his life until he has a chance to talk with you again.

"Miriam, he needs to be able to say these things to you—not to me.   I can't tell you what to do.   You are a woman now.   I just want you to know that I realize these are new times.   Good marriages are going to take on a different look in your generation and those to follow.   My marriage to Pa suited the times.   We struggled to make ends meet and raised strong sons and daughters to tame the land, but the pioneer days are gone and that's all right.   Your father worked so hard to make life better and different for his children, and it is up to each of you to make this world your own just the way he did. I made Dave no promises, Miriam, other than I would talk with you."

The next Sunday when Dave called in the sleigh after church, he received a warm welcome from Ma, Tildy, and the boys. Dave gave an audible gasp when Miriam appeared at the top of the stairs and made her way down to his side. It was awkward, but a heavy weight had been lifted off all the shoulders in the room. The family gave the couple all the uninterrupted time they needed to quietly begin to rebuild their relationship on solid ground. David and Miriam held hands on the settee, and the family was gratified to hear soft laughter emanate from the parlor from time to time.

Dave did not overstay his welcome. He had learned a thing or two from this experience and was acting more like a man than the overeager, lovesick boy he had been. Of all his experiences, this near loss of something dear to him had made a lasting impression, and he had learned lessons he would carry the rest of his life. Christmas Day came and went. The couple exchanged simple gifts: a woolen scarf for Dave and a leather-bound copy of the *Counties of Whitley and Noble Indiana* for

Miriam. Dave wanted her to have the weighty book which contained a written tribute to both her father and older brother as two of the best farmers and men of integrity in Smith Township. He had saved money from his fur sales to pay the princely sum of $15—a fortune for a book. Miriam considered the book a great treasure and placed it in a prominent spot on the mantelpiece for all to admire.

CHAPTER 14 1884

Dave's visit on the last day of the year was a special occasion. He harnessed his best horse with care and set out in the middle of the day to call on Miriam. She had assured him the family didn't have any special plans, and she would be home that day. Dave had promised her a sleigh ride, and she was looking forward to it on this white sparkling day. The sun glistened off pristine snowdrifts, and the horse trotted with head high, invigorated by the fresh air and sunshine. Off they glided, smooth as silk. Sliding around the corners threw them together, and Dave put his strong arm around Miriam's shoulder to anchor her safely next to his side. He had a joke saved up for her. Mark Twain had recently written: "A man who carries a cat by the tail learns something he can learn in no other way." They laughed at the popular author's cleverness, their breath sending puffs into the air. Dave was taking a different run today, down a county road she didn't know well. Rows of splintered corn stobs, remnants of the harvest, poked from the drifts and receded into the distance on both sides; corn shocks dotted the fields like so many Indian teepees, havens for the small animals in the winter. Field mice, rabbits, and hungry foxes investigated them each day. Their tracks crisscrossed and wove together like the stitching on a far-reaching white cotton quilt.

Miriam lifted her hand and pointed as they approached a beautiful stand of mature pines on their right. The snow lay in soft mounds on the branches, and crows cawed in excitement and wheeled about as the strangers approached. "Dave, look at those lovely pines. They remind me of my pine stand in front of our house. Pa used to encourage me to sit and think under those pines, something I haven't done for a long time. He called my new ideas my 'pine tree revelations.'"

Dave pulled back on the reins, spoke gently to the horse, and they came to a stop, runners creaking on the cold snow, in front of the pines. A light breeze caused some snowflakes to sift down on their shoulders, and the unexpected chill made both of them shiver and then smile. Dave suddenly hopped from the sleigh and held his hands up for Miriam. She was sure glad she had foregone fashion and worn her high warm boots today. He swung her down from the buggy, his hands encircling her waist. He took her gloved hand in his and led her off the road and up the bank until they were in a veritable cathedral of pines. Dave brushed the snow from a cut stump and seated her on it. It was his turn to say his piece, and he had gone over the words time and time again since Miriam had allowed him back into her life. He knelt before her in the snow so he could look her right in the eyes.

"Miriam, I am thankful you have allowed us this wonderful year to rebuild our friendship. You told me in my father's barn that I was listening to a grown woman. Well, at this moment, you are listening to a grown man. I pledge to be true to you my whole life through, to love you no matter what comes our way. I need your friendship and love. I desperately hope that you will allow me to be your partner in all things, to stand by you, to do whatever is best for you, and to put your happiness and peace of mind above my own. There is only one thing you need to know before you make up your mind, and I must make myself clear. I need two things in my life: you and the land. Please do not make me choose between them. Miriam, if you will have me, will you live with me on the land—not just any land—*this* land we are standing on right now? This very pine grove and 100 acres is mine. I signed the papers yesterday. I will plan to build a house on this very spot starting tomorrow, and you and I will make it our home, if you will only pledge to me this is what you want."

Miriam's answer was ready on the tip of her tongue. This last year of courting had convinced her that Dave was a young man of integrity. She loved Whitley County. Her roots were here—and she loved Dave. Her father would have approved of him for his strength, intellect, and breeding as the grandson of a true old settler and now owner of this good flat piece of fertile ground. She raised her dark eyes and looked into his. He was a man, not a boy, and he had earned her trust and friendship forever. She smiled and nodded. He lifted her off her feet and swung her around in joy. They slid down the bank, laughing, and headed off to share the news.

"Ma, she's going to marry her 'chicken coop' boy!" Dave flung the door open and swept in carrying Miriam into the kitchen and setting her down with a flourish. He grabbed Ma and Tildy in turn and did an exaggerated waltz with them. Evan and Frank joined in the hullabaloo, and Ma gave her permission to bring in the jug for a toast to the happy couple. The fire burned bright in the fireplace, and the family gathered around to raise their glasses high. What joy to have Dave back in the fold. Ma wished Pa could personally add his famous Irish toast to the happy occasion, but she remembered it well:

"May love and laughter light your days,
And warm your heart and home.
May good and faithful friends be yours,
Wherever you may roam.
May peace and plenty bless your world
With joy that long endures.
May all life's passing seasons
Bring the best to you and yours!"

Dave and Miriam flew out of the living room in a whirlwind of coats, hats, and skirts on their way to tell the news to the Pences, who had been very careful in the last year to allow the couple lots of time to determine their own future. This happy occasion would be Miriam's first visit back to the brick house. She was too excited to be nervous about her reception this time. Her heart and mind were entirely at ease at her decision to accept Dave's proposal.

Miriam received a warm embrace and understanding smile from Alice immediately upon entering the front door this time. Florence helped her off with her wraps and gave Dave a grin and peck on the cheek in her delight at his good sense and good fortune. Mr. Pence put aside his paper, arose from his reading chair, and came forward to give her a hug. His beard tickled her face as he gathered both her and Dave in his long, lanky arms. "I am so glad to welcome you to the family, Miriam. I hope you will feel free to call me Father or JJ." She knew from the sincerity of his words she was starting over with this family. Every bit of awkwardness was relinquished to the past. All was well.

The scene around the supper table was very different this evening. Miriam helped to set the table for five. Dave and Father sat at the parlor table by lamplight and inspected the survey of Dave's farm. They talked about fencing, ditches, and woodlots, and Miriam could see the excitement in Dave's eyes. The family enjoyed an intimate, unhurried dinner. Miriam confidently joined into the conversation. She loved watching their faces as she described Clover: her beauty, her cleverness, and her good health. Father got a thoughtful look in his eye and said that he had something he wanted to show her after supper, if she would agree to accompany him to the barn.

Standing in one of the stalls was a beautiful bay mare, her head lowered, her breathing labored. Father said she had been suffering from a cold and cough for three days, and he was getting very worried. The veterinarian had gone to visit family in Indianapolis for the holidays, and he was about to call upon her brother, George, for advice. Had George taught her how to treat Clover for this sort of malady?

He would be obliged, if she could think of anything to help. Miriam asked if he had a pencil handy. He produced a pencil and a small tablet he kept in the barn for figuring. She thought for a moment and then began to write out her older brother's blood purifier for horses. Father watched with a gratified expression as she bent her head over the lined paper and wrote in careful script, as if she were taking an exam in school:

"Blood Purifier Medicine

Mix together:

2 ½ oz. gentian root, pulverized

2 oz. sassafras bark

2 oz. elecampane (horseheal) roots and petals

1 oz. skunk cabbage, dried

1 oz. cream of tartar

2 ½ oz. nitrate of potash,

2 oz. pulverized ginger root,

6 oz. sulphur

1 oz. digitalis (powdered dried leaves of the foxglove)

1 oz. bloodroot,

1 oz. of dried and pulverized birch leaves"

She continued to write: "If your horse is in bad health, give a teaspoonful twice a day in bran mash. To prevent all internal diseases, give one tablespoonful in spring and fall once a day for 15 or 17 days. This receipt is to be given to horses twice a year, in spring and fall. This will keep your horses from having distemper, coughs, colds, heaves, or farey and keep them in good health."

She told Father that if she were at home, she could go into her mother's kitchen closet filled with dried herbs and roots and make up this cure in just a few moments, but she didn't know if Alice would have very many of these ingredients on hand.

She and Father re-entered the house, and, with booming voice, he made a grand pronouncement. "Everyone, this house is pretty dead for New Year's Eve. How would you like to have a house full of company tonight, Alice? It's short notice, but high time we welcomed Miriam's family into our home. She just gave me a good idea. Dave, hitch up the sleigh and take Miriam home right now...but turn around as quick as you can and bring her Ma and the boys back to spend the night with us. Tildy is welcome, too. How 'bout it, Miriam? Would they like to come? Should we do this betrothal up right?"

It was pretty irregular, but the Coulters all jumped at the chance to get together with the Pences. The boys wanted to see the big house, and New Year's Eve with the pretty and eligible Florence would be a highlight, too. Ma was flustered at the invitation, but Dave shooed her upstairs to pack her nightclothes. Tildy deferred and offered to tend the fire and do the morning chores so the family didn't have to rush back. She said she would relish a quiet evening with just herself, a warm fire, and her needlework for company—that luxury had rarely presented itself in all her born days. For that favor, Miriam danced her around the kitchen. She also took a few moments, under Ma's watchful eye, to carefully measure and mix the blood purifier medicine. The medicine, one of Tildy's pies, and a holiday fruitcake would have to be their contribution to the party on such short notice. Perhaps these Germans were not so different from the Irish, after all.

Chapter 15 1885

It was a warm June day. Miriam saddled Clover and rode at a brisk trot to meet Dave at his property. Clover's ears perked up when she heard her lady happily singing, "She'll be coming 'round the mountain when she comes!" Miriam brought a picnic lunch to savor in the shade of the pines: fruit, little crusty loaves of bread, and sheep's milk cheese infused with rosemary. She and Ma had been experimenting with cheeses from both cow's and sheep's milk. Some were better than others, and sometimes Evan rolled his eyes and comically stuck out his tongue after a sampling session. He still preferred grape jam on his bread.

Dave brought the plans for the house. He and Miriam had worked on them side by side all winter since the joyous engagement get-together, which had been declared a great success from both sides. Ma, Alice, and Florence suggested to Miriam that a New Year's Eve wedding at the Merriam Christian Chapel would make for a wonderful night; plus, Florence added with a smile, Dave could never forget their anniversary that way.

Miriam was letting Ma handle

wedding arrangements. She really wasn't very interested in the ceremony. It was the house that consumed her every waking moment. She learned very early that her husband-to-be came from stock that worked within a budget. His Scottish Waugh parents on his mother's side knew how to pinch a penny, according to Dave. That's why both the Waughs and the Pences had money to spare in the bank. It might be that they would have to wait for a while to have every little thing she wanted, but he would see that she got it. That was part of his pledge to her. He was going to build the house first and plan for a large bank barn to come sometime in the next decade. Dave and his father had determined that cattle would do well on his acres, so he was looking into the new Scottish Angus breed, which had been thriving in Indiana and providing a profitable living for some of the local farmers. It would take him a while to set aside enough money for the barn, but it was his one desire to paint his name in dignified letters above big white sliding doors.

The couple designed a very pretty home, inside and out. It would maximize interior space by being tall and rather stately for a white frame house. No bumping her head on the rafters in *these* upstairs rooms. The siding would be narrow clapboard and there would be two stories and an attic for storage. The house would sit right off the dirt county road, facing west for the afternoon and evening light in the front rooms. The morning sun would stream into the kitchen and back bedrooms on the east side, but those rooms would cool down during the heat of the day. The plans showed four upstairs bedrooms: two large and two small. All the upstairs rooms would be finished with plastered walls and doors exiting into a main hallway. A narrow, steep stairway would lead down into the living room. Ma was fashioning a heavy burgundy velveteen curtain to hang at the bottom of the stairs. Guests would enter through a front door featuring an ornate screen door installed in the summer. The drawing of the front porch showed four square pillars and a simple railing where Miriam could place pots planted with geraniums and vines. The porch roof was flat with a railing around it, as well. Dave said he saw a picture in a book that called the porch and pillars Italianate Style—sort of fancy—just for her. She approved. Twelve panes of glass would bring in light from each casement window. Miriam wanted lots of fresh air to circulate around the upper bedrooms on hot Indiana nights. By opening one window downstairs, pulling aside the curtain, and opening the windows a crack in all the bedrooms, the cool evening breezes would be pulled into the whole upstairs. If they positioned the beds just right, their children and guests would sleep comfortably.

The downstairs plans featured a large bedroom off the parlor. Miriam envisioned a cannonball cherry bed topped by embroidered linens and a marble-topped dressing table along one wall. Completing the main floor would be a front parlor, a living room with fireplace, the kitchen, and a pantry. A small bedroom for the help would be located in a half-story addition off to the south. The focal point of the kitchen was to be the most modern cook stove available from Detroit, the Stove Capital of the World. There would be built-in cupboards and a pump at the sink. It was going to be very convenient to have water handy for cooking and drinking, eliminating the need to fill and to carry sloshing buckets from the outside well.

Dave said he would need help with the farming, so he planned to hire a man and wife to live in to relieve Miriam from having to do the daily cooking. She was thankful for that kindness and promised him she would have Tildy give her a baking lesson and learn to make her famous old-fashioned cream pie. Mastering pie-baking would give Miriam a reason to appreciate this wonderful modern kitchen Dave was installing and also one dish to always take to the church suppers that she could truthfully claim to be made by her own hands.

Miriam's special room was going to be the parlor. She wanted a place where she could retreat to do her needlework and reading. This room would show off some of the wedding presents they would get from relatives far and near, maybe some gifts from as far as her grandparents in Ohio. She already owned a blue and white woven jacquard coverlet called Peacocks on the Nest, which had been woven in Ohio in 1843 by an itinerate weaver named J Hart. This special coverlet had been in Ma's hope chest and had come with them in the covered wagon before she was even born. Now it was nestled into her cedar chest. Maybe that was why Ma was so crazy about her peacocks. Miriam would bring her favorite quilt Ma had made her when she was but a child. It was mostly green and red and was appliquéd in the Rose of Sharon design. Ma had explained to her that the flowering shrub of that name was mentioned in the Bible as a symbol of immortality—even as a description of Christ, Himself. This special childhood possession had given her warmth and comfort for so many years, and she was looking forward to enjoying it in her own home.

Dave designed an ingenious eavestrough system that would gather the rain from the roof and run it down an angled pipe and into an underground cistern next to the drive. They could pump that nice soft rainwater to use for the garden—and to wash hair. Miriam was pleased. She would have never thought of that. Growing up, they had always just dipped soft water from a simple rain barrel at the back door for hair washing.

Dave and Miriam set the plans aside, held hands, and dreamed for a while under the pines. They gazed at the spot where, in their snug home, they would be living as man and wife in six short months. Instead of having the neighbors raise this house, it was the German tradition to bring in a crew of house builders, who would live on the property for as long as it took to get it enclosed. Building was about to begin. Jim's farm adjoined to the north, and they were glad to have so much loving Pence family close by.

The house was a gift from Father and Alice to the young couple, and Miriam felt very grateful to them. A life free of debt and housekeeping appealed to Miriam, and Ma was constantly amazed at the special treatment the Pences rained down upon her daughter. Some of their largesse spilled over onto her and her family, too. When Frank married that year, the Pences gave him some Angus breeding stock for his farm. They had just begun to experiment with this hornless, black breed from Scotland, and it was doing well in the Indiana climate. Miriam and Dave presented him with a henhouse and a dozen Wyandotte chickens. Frank married a girl with whom Miriam didn't have much in common, but he seemed happy, and his new wife wasn't too demanding. That just left Evan at home with Ma, and he took care of the chores, farmed Ma's and his 160 combined acres, and seemed as if he would be a bachelor forever. After all, he could come home to a hot meal and a warm bed every night and go out with any girl he wanted on the weekends when his chores were done. He cut a handsome figure in his shiny buggy pulled by a well-groomed black horse.

Miriam and Dave would raise corn on the eighty acres she had inherited from Pa. They could use Pa's old equipment to get the seed in the ground, and they would reap the benefits of the harvest in fodder for their herd. There were increasingly hard feelings about the division of the original homestead among her siblings since affordable land in the area was becoming harder to find. Evan was criticized for taking advantage of Ma's good graces. Miriam's brothers and sister were suspicious he would end up with the house and more than his share of everything after her death. Sis complained that she and her husband needed more acres and that the boys had unfairly inherited more than the girls. Ma was caught in the crossfire and came to Evan's defense, which made the hard feelings even worse. Pa did not make his plans clear to the children before his death, and Miriam found herself drawn more and more intimately into Dave's solid, friendly family.

To add to the upheaval, Tildy had gotten a letter from her family in Ohio. Her mother was seriously ill, and, as the only single woman of the family, she was needed to help with her aging father. In return for Tildy's help, her brothers and sisters promised her the house and ten acres of the homestead after his death. The rest would be sold, and careful investment of her equal part would give her a life income. Tildy felt compelled to answer that call. It was a sad day when she climbed onto the train that would take her away. Ma and Miriam were the only ones to see her off. Evan had driven them into town but had disappeared to the livery stable to visit with the men.

This simple farewell didn't seem like a befitting way for the children to express their gratitude for all her years of service and friendship. Tears were shed as the porter lifted her trunk into the storage car. Tildy squared her shoulders, embraced both women in turn, gave Miriam her blessing and climbed aboard. The steam whistle sounded a mournful note that afternoon, and a chapter in the lives of the Coulters was closed forever.

Chapter 16 1885

December 31 dawned bright and clear, reminiscent of the couple's engagement day exactly one year before. But the winter scene at the pine grove had undergone a transformation. A pristine two story farmhouse stood beyond the snow-laden pines. Snow had drifted around the front porch, and the many windowpanes sparkled with frost. The finishing touches were all in place to welcome the newly-weds home after the ceremony and reception at Miriam's church.

The two families and friends converged on the little brick church in their sleighs, bells jingling, befitting the holiday spirit. The women disembarked at the church door, and the men and boys congregated in the field beyond where they put blankets on the horses and hitched them to the rails. The men stayed outside, visiting and looking over each other's rigs with admiration. The groom arrived just a little bit late—his harness decked out in shiny silver studs. Copper bells of four different sizes hanging from his harness rang out a greeting. The men welcomed him with great hurrahs, and he blushed at their greeting. What a life, and what a great future! Here he was, twenty years old with a house soon to become a home when he carried his wonderful Miriam over the threshold tonight. He was the luckiest, most invincible man in the world.

The guests filled every pew. Reverend Miller greeted the congregation and first led them all in prayer. The young couple rose and went forward. They joined hands and the minister quietly spoke of the sanctity of marriage and of God's love. Miriam was listening, but she also was studying this man she was joining in a lifetime partnership. She seemed to see him with a new clarity. He had dark eyes like hers, a prominent nose, and his ears stuck out even more since his wedding haircut. His facial expression was firm, but his cool damp hands betrayed his nervousness. Dave gazed at his little bride, as well. Miriam wore a dark wool skirt. Her jacket had a line of mother-of-pearl buttons up the front. She wore a blouse with a high collar, a gold necklace, and a small pocket watch with a chain and fob was pinned at her waist, a gift from her brothers. Miriam had told him she was going to follow the tradition of something old: the birdstone in a small slash pocket in her skirt; something new: her gold watch; something borrowed: a gold necklace from her mother; and something blue: a baby blue handkerchief tucked into the end of one sleeve. Her dark hair was pulled back severely in a bun at the nape of her neck, but a pretty wavy hairpiece framed her face with curls. Ma had made the white taffeta and lace bonnet that would be put into a special box and kept as a keepsake after the wedding. Miriam's mouth was serious. Her eyes looked deeply into his with love and trust. She had beautiful deep eyes and strong brows. Her body was small but shapely. He and she made a perfect match. Dave was as sure of that as anything he had ever known in his life. He slipped the gold band on her finger to symbolize their everlasting love, and it was done. Miriam was a Pence, now.

The couple beamed at their guests, and everyone gathered around. All present heard the comforting rustle of skirts and the familiar squeaks of the church plank floor underfoot, and they all noticed the fragrance of the evergreen boughs that graced the altar. A simple repast of punch and spice cake was served. As Miriam and Dave swept out of the churchyard to the cheers and waves of the crowd, Miriam glimpsed Ma slowly walking alone through the drifts toward Pa's grave.

Chapter 17   1886

Miriam and Dave were snug in their new home that winter. They closed the heavy drapery at the bottom of the stairs, leaving the upstairs unheated, and put their belongings in the downstairs bedroom that was warmed by the parlor stove, which would be moved out of the way into the shed for storage every spring. Dave kept the home fires burning, and they spent the winter enjoying each other's company: reading, preparing simple meals together, receiving their first guests, and going to Father's house for Sunday dinner. Miriam insisted they attend the Merriam Christian Chapel, so she could see her mother every weekend. Ma seemed to be getting along all right at home. She had hired a young woman named Sal to help her around the place, and that seemed to be working out well. Sal was only sixteen and didn't have Tildy's cooking skills, but she was good company. Ma was nearing sixty and didn't get around as well as she used to.

As spring came on, Dave made preparations for hiring help, planned his planting schedule, and traveled with his father to the Fort Wayne stockyards to select his breeding cattle. Miriam sometimes left her new husband to his preoccupations, bundled up in her wool coat, saddled Clover, and rode over to spend a day or so with Ma during the week. Clover relished the chance to get out after the long winter. She carried her mistress with great care, however, and kept a steady, smooth stride over the muddy roads. Miriam loved these jaunts. She would sometimes stop Clover to watch the does with their spotted fawns peek their heads from the margins of the woodlands and come forward to taste the new blades of grass sprouting by the roadside.

She looked forward to starting her own garden. Ma promised to have cuttings, seeds, and small plants for her to bring home—even a nice tuber from the old, reliable pie plant. She had rosemary, thyme, dill, and the medicinal herbs ready and waiting to go into her kitchen garden. Father had promised to take her on a morel mushroom hunt on his land along the Blue River. He claimed to have quite an eye for spotting the brown, wrinkled delicacies among the leaves and forest litter. There was much to look forward to this spring.

Miriam's thoughts were thus preoccupied, and she nearly rode past Ma's lane, but Clover knew her destination and did the turning for her. Evan was out in the barnyard and kindly offered to tend Clover and put her out to pasture. He and Miriam shared a hug. She couldn't get too angry at him for staying a bachelor. It just didn't seem to be in his nature to get tied down to one girl. He was in his mid-thirties, enjoyed spending time with the other men at the lodge in Churubusco, and tramping his trap line. He did a fair to middling job at farming the land. Miriam felt her other brothers were too critical of Evan. Miriam had always had a soft spot in her heart for Evan and knew that Ma did, too.

Ma met her at the door, and she hung her coat on the top row. She wistfully considered all those coat hooks, bottom row empty. She suspected why she seemed to feel so nostalgic of late—even Dave had mentioned that he was having a hard time getting her to laugh with his little tricks, jokes, and teasing. She knew he loved to see those flashing Irish eyes—and he also liked to gaze on her contented face by the fire in the evenings. What a great friend and companion he was, and what a wonderful thing to spend the whole winter with just him by the fire. It had been a wonderful, long honeymoon for them both.

Ma brewed some peppermint tea and they sat down to visit. Sal had gone to see her older sister for a couple of days, so Evan and Ma were shifting for themselves. Miriam took Ma's hands in her own and quietly told her that her menses had stopped. She had reread Dr. Chase's chapters on pregnancy, and she was sure that she showed all the early symptoms. She was happy, amazed, and frightened, all at the same time. Miriam had told no one about her condition, not even Dave. She needed Ma to know first.

Ma looked closely at her youngest child. Miriam's dark eyes had welled with tears, and Ma certainly knew just how she felt. She gathered her daughter into her arms and held her tightly as Miriam cried, and she thought of the day back in Ohio when her mother held her just so. She had barely turned nineteen when she felt their first born George quicken. It had been a moment made more poignant by the fact they were preparing to leave to unknown territories, and Miriam's mother would only see the baby as a toddler, and rarely be part of her daughter's life again, through all eleven pregnancies and births. At least she could be sure that Miriam and this grandchild would be a Whitley County child born and bred. She could be part of the lives of Miriam's children.

Miriam's sobs subsided, and the two women shared a light supper and talked late into the night. Ma told Miriam all she had experienced in her own pregnancies, lying in, and the confinement period following each one. Miriam's confidence was raised. What a wonderful mother. Ma knew just how to quell her fears. Ma had assured her that, if she took precautions, kept getting exercise, fresh air, and good food, and didn't listen to anyone who told her she needed bed rest and coddling, she would safely bring a new little life into the world. And, make no doubt about it, Ma would be there by her side until she could put the dear one safely into her arms. Ma encouraged her to continue to ride Clover until July, but then she should take out the buggy instead. Miriam was heartened. She had life stirring in her womb. Wait until she told her unsuspecting Dave. Just the thought of his startled reaction made her smile. Maybe his son's ears would stick out, too. Maybe he would have Pa's beautiful voice.

CHAPTER 18 1886

In the golden waning light, Dave and Miriam stood side by side looking out over their fields with pride. Dave wore blue denim pants and a grey cotton store-bought shirt, sleeves rolled to the elbows. His dark, weary eyes peered out from under a gray felt hat with a wide brim, the band sweat-stained and faded from the sun. His arms were tanned and his body was lean and wiry. Black suspenders held up his pants. His hair rubbed against his collar; he needed a haircut but had no time for that. He and the hired man had been working before dawn to dusk for weeks during the harvest. When he saw his suit hanging on the peg at bedtime, he knew he would awaken to the Sabbath and have a welcome day of rest. Miriam would be sure of that. His right arm rested gently over Miriam's shoulders, and she had her thumb hooked into his left suspender at his waist. She wore a dress her mother had made for her. It was combed cotton with a small navy stripe. It featured a high waist to modestly conceal the swell of her pregnancy under the long pleated skirt. Ma had made her three of these dresses suitable for church-going even in her condition, but last Sunday had been her final appearance at church and in town until the baby would arrive early in the new year and they would bring him or her to church for christening. Until then, her visits would be restricted to family.

Dave looked fondly down at Miriam. His hard work had paid off this summer. The cows were settled in, bred, and ready to calve next spring. The mucky soil had not disappointed him. Even his father exclaimed over the quantity and quality of his crops. That great praise warmed his heart. The couple he had hired to help them in the house, garden, and fields had turned out to be wonderful, trustworthy, hard-working people, glad for the opportunity. His bank account was growing. His dear wife carried their first child and looked beautiful in her pregnancy. Miriam's hair was shiny, her body had taken on new curves, and she seemed happy and confident about this great undertaking of bearing and raising a child. Accommodations for the little one had been planned, and Alice had brought down a pine rocking cradle that had been stored up in the attic of the old house for who knows how long. It would work perfectly for the first few months. Jim was a very good young father, and Dave had been paying attention to him—taking lessons.

They had chosen a doctor to attend Miriam. It unnerved Dave to know the baby was due in the dead of winter, but Jim had pledged to battle even the stormiest weather to get the doctor to them in time. Ma would come down to stay for a week or so beforehand. That gave him some comfort.

He was a lucky, lucky man. He would join his brothers and sisters in bringing a fourth generation of Pence blood into Whitley County. He had recently read in the paper of a journalist who claimed they were all living in something he called The Golden Years and wrote, "Ain't God good to Indiana, Ain't He Fellers? Ain't He though?" Yes, Dave agreed, God seemed to be looking down in special favor to this place.

Miriam loved feeling her strong husband's arm across her shoulders and the kick of new life in her swollen belly. She could finally understand how her mother felt each of those eleven times she and Pa had brought life into this world. It was a privilege and responsibility she meant to take seriously. She looked forward to meeting this little child who kicked and hiccupped, disturbing her sleep, but making her smile through the discomfort. She encouraged Dave to feel the kick under his big rough hand. He worked up the nerve to do it and declared with a laugh and a blush, "This child must have a lot of the Irish in him because he is already doing a jig!"

Of the whole Pence family, Miriam had established an easy, comfortable relationship with Father. She admired his determination to get his hands on any new information to make the family more progressive farmers. He read the newspapers and farm journals cover to cover and would share what he had learned with her. Ever since she cured his brown mare with her blood purifier, he showed his respect to her more than to any of the others who had married into the family. She did not feel like a traditional daughter-in-law; she loved him in mutual admiration as a daughter. It delighted Miriam to realize this imposing man, who had all but chased her off the first time she met him, had become her trusted male mentor and friend.

Dave had to smile when he would come in the back door and find all the other women in the kitchen, except for Miriam. She could always be found sitting at Father's side on the settee in animated conversation. She was an attentive audience for his tales of his father, George. Father revered his Pa the way Miriam revered hers, and they laughed and talked until dinner was on the table. Miriam would glide into the dining room on

Father's arm and would charm them with her quick wit and ability to recite bits and pieces of poetry and song. She was a feisty one. He remembered her staunch support of his sister Florence, who expressed a desire to attend Valparaiso University after she finished her high school education. Miriam flew into apoplexy when he mentioned to her that he and the rest of the family thought his sister was tetched in the head to consider such a plan. Miriam demanded Dave drive them down to the old house immediately so she could stand up for Florence. That was a fuss. But, after the dust cleared, Florence packed her bags the next fall and set off to study business, and, by golly, she fell in with a boy studying law and was now back in Columbia City—a lawyer's wife—with a nice house in town, a baby, and more invitations to the ladies' societies than she could ever think of accepting. Dave guessed this must be the Golden Years for women, too.

Chapter 19 1886

Miriam's pregnancy was celebrated by the Pence family. Alice and Father loved to see her on Sundays, and, since she was "confined," she and Dave sometimes went over to the brick house in the mornings after Dave's chores were done in order to have a full day with family. On those occasions, Dave lent Father a hand with his livestock and completed the necessary equipment repairs. Until Dave had the funds to build his "dream" barn, he was sharing workhorses and farming implements with his father, and he took his maintenance responsibilities seriously. Relieving his father from those dirty chores was the least he could do to uphold his part of the bargain. Miriam's tending of the horses was welcome, even in her condition, and the horses had become fond of her visits. She spoke softly and always brought them a carrot or even an occasional lump of sugar, and they stood stock-still under her probing hands. She checked their skin condition, eyes, and teeth, looked over their legs and hooves carefully, and reported back to Father. She remembered Pa's statement that horses were the farmer's living tools and deserved loving care. She was proud that Father took such good care of his workhorses. Some of the local farmers used them harshly and fed them poorly. When a horse was abused and all played out, the tallow man would come and lead him away to be put down, skinned, and rendered into products Miriam would rather not think about.

When JJ would carry two wicker chairs off the porch and place them under the pines where he could see the Blue River and have a view of his fields and barn, Miriam knew he was in the mood to tell her some stories of the old days. He would light up a cigar, and she would pull her shawl about her shoulders, settle her unwieldy body into the cushions of the comfortable chair, and listen:

"Miriam, I trace my family back to Nicolas Pence in Germany. Philip Pence, his son, came from there as a young man to Virginia around the time of the War for Independence. He traveled west, mostly by waterways, and settled on a farm in Highland County, Ohio, down by the Ohio River. Tragedy struck Philip one day as he was bringing a load of corn on the ferry across the river. The boat sprang a leak about halfway over and began to sink. Since he could not swim, Nicolas tried to jump on the back of one of his horses in order to ride to safety, but the horse kicked out in fear. Philip was stunned and drowned right there on the spot. The river swept him away. I give him great respect because he was the one to take the risk to venture west.

"My father George, Philip's son, was an older man when I was born. He had married Sarah Windel, a gal from the beautiful Shenandoah Valley. He was forty years older than I, but he sure had a lot of spirit. He sold his Ohio land in 1836 and headed north with us nine children—six boys and three girls—in a covered wagon pulled by a massive pair of oxen. I was the youngest, five years old at the time, and well remember the adventure through the wilderness. I recall sitting, wide-eyed, next to Mother on the seat of the covered wagon or napping on a cushion directly behind her. Father was determined to get to his property through the hardwood forests, and there were no roads at the time. We met Miami and Potawatomi hunters along the way, and Father tried to communicate in friendly gestures. We were all frightened by the sounds and glimpses of lean and hungry wolves circling through the woods around our nightly campfires. Father and Henry kept their rifles handy at all times. We never lacked for vittles; there was plenty of wild game for eating: deer, wild pigs, and turkey. Three of my brothers are still in Whitley County: Henry, Abraham, and John. Henry was twenty-four, Abe eighteen, and John thirteen when we came to Indiana, so you know a lot of the work fell to them. They worked side by side with my father to clear a wagon's width of road to get us to this very spot, Section 19 of Smith Township. This whole section belonged to Father. He paid $1,200 for the 640 acres, and we were bound to get here all in one piece, if he could help it. We all jumped in to help once Father felled the big trees with his axe or crosscut saw. The oxen were hitched up to skid the logs out of the way. My job was to clear the small branches from the roadway so they could not damage the wagon wheels or the oxen's legs. Those strong animals meant our survival, and we could not afford to have one injured. Mother and my oldest sister Eliza would cook our meals by campfire. The boys would cut the saplings and help to position the medium-sized logs into a corduroy road over the swampy spots—and there were lots of swampy spots back in those days before we dug all these drainage ditches.

"There were no bridges across the streams or the swamps, as there are now. The streams were frequently swollen by the heavy rains, and we could not wait for the water to subside. It was often impossible for the team to draw the loaded wagon through the streams, so then it was necessary to fell a tree across the stream at some point where it was narrow enough for the tree to reach well across. We would unload our wagon and carry everything across; then Father would drive the team through with the empty wagon. Since I couldn't swim, I got to sit by Father as we attempted the crossing. If the stream was too deep, we would swim our team through, push our wagon into the stream as far as we could, fasten long ropes to the end of the tongue, hitch the team to it on the other side, pull the wagon through, let the wagon dry out overnight, grease the wheels, reload, and resume our journey. Once in a while the commotion would attract settlers from an isolated cabin. The families would rejoice at the sounds of friendly voices and would join us for supper and a visit. Father and Mother often left the remainders from our meal with these people, who sometimes seemed desperate for both sustenance and company.

"It was exhausting work to take a wagon where no wheels had ever gone before, but we made it. The work wasn't done once we got here, though. We had wanted to build a cabin to shelter us from the coming winter, but the snow this far north took us by surprise well before Thanksgiving Day. We stripped the canvas off our wagon and made a lean-to tent that served as a place to huddle while the men and oxen struggled in a foot of snow and frigid temperatures to cut and haul suitable logs for our house. Willis and Absalom managed to kill enough game to keep us from starving, but my mother told me later that she was reaching a point of desperation to keep eleven mouths fed. My mother sacrificed part of her every portion so I would not go without.

"Despite the trials and tribulations, Father loved this very spot where we are sitting and saw its potential as a home site. He retained his pioneer zeal, and his enthusiasm was contagious. To a little boy like me, our life of privation was all an adventure and a game. To my parents and older brothers and sisters, getting established here had to have felt like sheer drudgery.

"After several years of back-breaking teamwork, we managed to clear some land in order to have a bit of pasture, a good garden, a snug house, and some chickens and pigs. Henry and the neighbor gal, Equilla Gradeless, were united in holy matrimony in the first wedding to be held in Thorncreek Township. In fact, their marriage was only the fourth recorded in the whole of Whitley County. Imagine that. Eliza's marriage to James Rousseau followed before too long. They lost their first baby, so Father gave half an acre of his land on the banks of the Blue River for a cemetery to be used by the township residents. I remember the little baby being laid to rest there and Father and Mother ever after calling it the Rousseau Graveyard in the little fellow's memory. My mother Sarah and my brother Absalom rest in peace there, as well. My brother Willis and all the others who have gone before take up a lot of space in another cemetery called the Gradeless Cemetery across from the church on the river. I'll lay my bones down there, too, some day, for eternal rest. You are bringing the new into the world, and we old folks just have to have enough sense to get out of the way sooner or later."

JJ paused a moment to get a fresh cigar out of his pocket. He bit off the end and struck the long sulfur match on the bottom of one of his Sunday shoes. He slowly puffed as Miriam watched the flame burn closer and closer to his fingers. Then, just in the nick of time, he shook the match out, rolled it between his thumb and index finger, and tossed it on the pine needles. She loved watching that ritual with bated breath.

"The Indians annoyed my father and

worried my mother. She had heard about children being kidnapped, told their parents were dead, and adopted into the tribes as either warriors or wives. The older children were charged to keep a close watch on us younger ones. Father and Mother didn't much mind when a Miami woman would silently pad on moccasin feet straight into our kitchen and hold out a deerskin bag for a handout of flour or sugar. It startled Mother to turn around with a hot pan off the stove only to confront an unfamiliar, stony-faced woman with a papoose on her back, but we were glad to share with anyone in need. What did anger Father, though, was their stealing our hogs. There were so many of us children, he probably would have noticed a missing hog faster than a missing child.

"One evening after our dinner, we heard the report of a rifle, and, despite Mother's protestations, Father grabbed his black powder rifle from its spot over the mantel and headed out into the dusk. He heard the barking of dogs and the squealing of hogs, so he headed out in the direction of the sounds. When he reached the spot, about a quarter mile from the house, he discovered a Miami in the act of drawing one of his hogs, which he had killed, up onto his pony. Father fired and missed him. The Miami abandoned his booty, gave a loud whoop, and galloped away. Father loaded his gun again and killed both the dogs that were still attacking his hogs.

"Abe had gone out to witness the event and to help Father, if he could, but he ran back in fear when he heard Father's shots. Abe herded us all down into the root cellar below the kitchen floor trapdoor and was poised at the top of the ladder with his own gun. He was rightly afraid of reprisal if the Indian had been killed. It wouldn't have been long before the rest of the tribe up at Seek's Village would have heard about this. We had been living on this land under a shaky truce with the native people, and it had not recently come to bloodshed in this neighborhood as it had down south of us on the Tippecanoe. We hoped, if they came for retribution, they would not set the house afire with us down under the floor.

"We heard Father cry out in concern when he banged the front door open and found us gone. Abe earned a hug of gratitude for his good, clear thinking about how to protect the family. Father, Mother, Abe, and John took turns standing guard all night. I sat with Ma as long as I could keep my eyes open. We stoked up the fire and all slept on the floor in the front room just in case we had to fight or run. The whole thing blew over, to the relief of the neighbors, who clapped Father on the back and thanked him for being a bad shot. We didn't want old John Turkey to start taking potshots at us. He was a pretty good Miami marksman and a mean one, who hung around the Columbia City area taverns.

"In those early days, we were not able to raise enough grain for ourselves and our animals, so we had to purchase corn and wheat from either the Elkhart prairie to the northwest, or sometimes we had to travel all the way to Fort Wayne. We counted ourselves fortunate if we could get to Fort Wayne and back in two days because of the swampy conditions. A million things could go wrong on the way and leave us stranded until we could ride out to some sort of settlement. We were glad when a water-powered grist mill and sawmill were erected on the Blue River. They weren't fancy operations, but they did allow us to keep from starving, and we could make some cash from our walnut and white oak to pay for milled lumber to build with. Imagine, Miriam, in part of the county back then, as much as $500 and even more could be realized from the walnut timber from just one acre of land alone.

"The first trader in the county was a Frenchman by the name of Francis Godfroy. He had a small store in his cabin southeast of Blue Lake. He mostly traded with the Indians, and his prices were accordingly inflated, so we were glad when Churubusco started to pop—and look at it now.

"My father took an interest in the justice system of this new land. After he became known hereabouts as a fair and intelligent man, he was named onto the petit court jury that met down in Columbia City, which had become the county seat by that time. There wasn't any courthouse yet, so the court met in a residence belonging to Richard Baughan. He got paid three dollars every time they used his house for court business. There was no sufficient separate room in which the jury could deliberate, so, usually, in good weather, they marched out to some convenient log, and, seating themselves upon it, they made up their verdict in the open air.

"After mother died, Father sent me to secure some land in Iowa. Everyone was making such a fuss about that newly opened territory. Word had come back about the thick prairie topsoil in the middle of the state where you didn't even have to cut down one tree to get started farming. Sounded good to me, and I was twenty-three and ready to have my own place, if I liked it out there. Father said maybe he would be ready to move on, too. He still had the wanderlust in him. Father had been giving my married brothers each eighty acres here and there, but I wanted more. I had just met the lovely, spirited, ambitious Susan Waugh, though, and I made her promise to wait for me to get back. She was only sixteen, and her parents were not in any hurry for her to marry, but we sure fancied one another right off. She allowed me to kiss her goodbye, and that sweet memory sustained me on my lonely trek.

"I rode off to Iowa on horseback, taking my time and looking over all the country between here and there. I forded small creeks and rivers and used the ferries on the big rivers. There were good stagecoach trails that led me to Hardin County, smack dab in the middle of the state. I was able to purchase 240 acres at a little more than a dollar an acre. I took several days to ride to Des Moines for supplies and to telegraph the news to my father—a new form of communication between us. I hoped getting a telegram delivered would be fun for the family. I know it was a thrill to write it down and listen to the operator tap out my message. I just imagined my words flying down that wire from pole to pole all the way back to Whitley County.

"I went about building a cabin and small barn for oxen that were needed to work the deep grasslands in this part of the country. Horses were not near strong enough to pull the plow through the heavy layer of sod. The surrounding farmers were having good luck with wheat, and the market was strong, so that is what I decided to grow. It would be impossible to fence the vast land because of the lack of timber for posts, so crops were better than livestock. Buffalo roamed the hills and vales and made for good eating. After only a year in that territory, increasingly overrun with new immigrants and Civil War veterans claiming their reward in the form of land grants, I got lonesome for Susan and missed this black Indiana soil. I hankered for a woodlot. I missed the sound of frogs in the spring and spending a lazy day at Round Lake under a tree with my fishing pole. I got homesick for the smell and sound of the leaves underfoot in the fall and the sparkle of the fireflies in the hot summer evenings. I closed up the place after the harvest and headed out on my horse again…only this time I headed into the morning sun. While I was sleeping by my fire, five nights into my journey, I heard a commotion. Three Indians on their ponies had taken the hobbles off my horse and were driving him out of sight over a ridge, whooping and laughing. I was in a predicament. I was trying to get home before the snow flew. I didn't want to lose my saddle, so I hoisted it up on my shoulder. You might not believe me when I tell you this, Miriam, but I arranged my knapsack and canteen across my chest and began to walk. I met a lot of good people on the way hoofing it back to the newly nicknamed Hoosier State. I didn't have cash money to buy a horse or mule, so I just kept on walking and stopped in with settlers along the way. They would give me a place to sleep in front of their fireplaces and usually shared their breakfasts with me for the company. The further I trekked east, the clearer the vision of sweet Susan's face became. When I first spotted the big ghostly sycamores along the banks of the Wabash, I'm not ashamed to say, I knelt down in tears and thanked God for bringing me home safe.

"I showed up back at the home place looking like something the cat dragged in. Father took me in his arms and welcomed me home, though. He and I talked for hours that night after I had a good soak in the copper washtub. That's when I decided to wear this beard the rest of my life. Even though I wasn't sure what Susan would think if these whiskers, I couldn't stand the thought of dragging a razor over my face even one more time. I headed off to see Susan in the morning, and her mother set to feeding me enough to make me almost bust. Afterward, I got down on my knee in the parlor and took Susan's soft hands in my rough ones. I told her I had made up my mind to stay in Smith Township for the rest of my life, and I had to have her for my wife. She accepted right away by giving me another one of those kisses, and her Father and Mother added their blessing. They both seemed impressed with the man I had become through my experiences and trials.

"I traded Father all the land in Iowa for 120 acres of the old place and chose a spot right next to the Blue River to build a cabin for Susan and me. We set right out having a family. Miriam, you know and love all my children—and they do you—except for little Nancy we lost at an early age.

"Father distributed the remaining acres to my other siblings, packed up his belongings in our old covered wagon, and we all bade him farewell as he headed off alone to Iowa. We got word from time to time that he liked it fine and had found a fine widow woman to marry. He lived out there with her for twelve years until he passed and left the farm to his wife. None of us could make it all the way out there to the funeral, but, now that I am an old man, I often think of my father resting out there on the prairie with wildflowers growing on his grave."

JJ's storytelling had wound down for the day. He and Miriam rose and they walked slowly across the road, arm in arm, to see how Dave was faring with his repair project. Dave welcomed them with a smile and held up the harness—leather conditioned and fragrant. His hands were dirty and his striped shirt had a polish stain that would be impossible to wash out. Miriam smiled and shook her head. This husband of hers—how she loved him. She also adored Father, who held her so protectively under the elbow and could be trusted to never let her fall.

Chapter 20 1886

Dave paced outside the closed bedroom door. Jim was there to give him some encouragement about being a father, but Dave's mind was on Miriam. He had heard her cry out in pain, and his heart ached so much he had to leave the house and go out and stand by himself among the cows in the cattle enclosure. It was cold comfort that all of those cows were carrying calves; he dreaded having to also witness the throes of birth with each of them. He had spent a lot of time tending the cows, and they welcomed his presence because it almost always meant an extra ration of hay and someone to break through the ice on the water trough. He stood, back against the fence, and watched them, bodies already swollen, lowing softly, chewing their cuds, jostling for a spot to drink. The smell of their warm bodies and the odor of manure were so familiar. His breathing slowed and he got his heartbeat under control. Dave knew it said in the Bible a woman must suffer to bring forth new life, but he sure thought that was a rough pronouncement. If he could just shoulder the pain in Miriam's stead, he would welcome it. He had never felt so helpless.

Jim called from the back door and beckoned to Dave. What? News? He leaped the fence and ran to the back steps, shedding his coat and muddy boots by the door. He stepped through the parlor in his stockinged feet and into the bedroom. Miriam was alive, that was certain. His knees were weak, and he knelt at the bed in a prayer of thanksgiving and because he could no longer stand. When he lifted his eyes, he found himself locked in a gaze with a tiny, wizened, red-faced creature that looked unlike anything he had ever seen. Miriam introduced him to his son, Evan.

Miriam was weak from the delivery and had lost a good deal of blood, but Ma and the doctor had been tending to her, and they were confident she was out of danger. Ma would take over from here, and the doctor gave her his profuse thanks for her capable assistance. He packed up his bag and left the room quietly, whispering to Ma in passing that the Pences were good for their money, and he would come to the house to see the little mother in three weeks' time. Dave could settle the bill with him then. Jim and the doctor headed back to Churubusco in Jim's sleigh.

Dave studied his son in wonder. He played with his nieces and nephews but had never been around a brand-spanking new baby before. He counted the pink fingers and ran his rough palm over the bald little head. Miriam gazed at Dave and then at the little miracle in her arms. They were now a family—and they felt it through and through. Dave was a little puzzled at her choice of the name Evan. Miriam's family was sort of down on her brother, though he didn't see anything in particular wrong with him. He had promised Miriam she could name the baby, though, so Evan it was and would always be. Miriam had told him she hoped the baby would be a boy who would have a beautiful voice like her father. Well, when little Evan Pence decided to haul off and hit a high note, both Miriam and Dave had to laugh. Dave hightailed it out of the room so Ma could teach Miriam how to suckle the new baby. That was surely not his department.

Chapter 21 1888

He was a good boy—a roly-poly boy—a little devilish sometimes, who reminded Miriam so much of her departed brother Willie. She had considered naming him after her father and brother but just couldn't be reminded of her losses every time she looked at her son. His ears did stick out and he had his father's high forehead. The Pences valued his baby fat— a round baby was a healthy baby in the German culture. He loved to visit the red brick house because he was constantly entertained in someone's arms, slipped little treats on the sly, and never had to nap. Those Sundays made him fussy during the week when he had to return to sitting with his blocks and other toys on the parlor floor. He pulled up and toddled about while his mother worked on her sewing, and he had to be watched very carefully. Dave fashioned a chicken wire guard to surround the parlor stove, and Miriam moved her few precious items out of his reach, when she found her milk-glass cat on the floor, ear broken. The baby had no fear and could climb onto the settee to reach the high shelf. He was never spanked when he got into mischief; his mother could not resist laughing at his impish grin. He loved to laugh and listen to his mother sing little ditties and recite her poems. He formed a few words: Da and Ma. Evan squirmed out of his father's grasp to cuddle up to his mother when she entered the room. At bedtime, a freshly bathed Evan in his nightclothes leaned back on her lap, and Miriam recited a favorite Dave had taught her. It was a poem by a Scottish man named McDonald and was the only memory Dave had of Susan, his true mother. When Dave was with them in the parlor, he put down his paper and listened to her, too, as she spoke softly and gently caressed her sleepy son.

"Where did you come from, baby dear?
Out of the everywhere into here.

Where did you get your eyes so blue?
Out of the sky as I came through.

What makes the light in them sparkle and spin?
Some of the starry spikes left in.

Where did you get that little tear?
I found it waiting when I got here.

What makes your forehead so smooth and high?
A soft hand stroked it as I went by.

What makes your cheek like a warm white
rose?
I saw something better than anyone knows.

Whence that three-cornered smile of bliss?
Three angels gave me at once a kiss.

Where did you get this pearly ear?
God spoke, and it came out to hear.

Where did you get those arms and hands?
Love made itself into hooks and bands.

Feet, whence did you come, you darling
things?
From the same box as the cherubs' wings.

How did they all just come to be you?
God thought about me, and so I grew.

But how did you come to us, you dear?
God thought about you, and so I am here."

By the time the poem was recited,
Evan was fast asleep and ready for his little
bed tucked in a cozy corner of their
bedroom. Miriam would carry him in and
Dave would pull back the down comforter
and then cover him to his chin. My, he was
a darling angel.

Miriam had broken the news to

Dave that he was going to be a father again. She had counted the months and figured they would be welcoming a second child into the family in August. Evan would have a sibling close in age. She was hoping for a girl this time to complete their family.

CHAPTER 22 1888

Once more, Ma assisted during Miriam's second delivery. Miriam had followed all the instructions for pregnant women in Dr. Chase's book, and she began her labor as a strong and healthy woman. He had recommended gardening and plenty of sunshine, so Miriam spent the summer with a barefooted, dusty Evan in tow cultivating both her kitchen garden of cooking and medicinal herbs and her large vegetable garden. She pulled tiny weeds on her hands and knees right up to the time when she felt the first pangs of labor and sent the hired woman to get Dave from the fields. She knew what to expect this time, and the doctor barely had time to arrive before she was ready to deliver a beautiful, healthy, blue-eyed daughter. She named her Lilah Mae.

As far as Miriam was concerned, her family was complete now. She and Dave had decided, if the new baby was a healthy girl, they would limit their family to two children. His brothers and sisters were rearing small families: two or three children, instead of the six, eight, or even eleven of the generation before. The old settlers needed many sons to help tame the

Indiana wilderness, and numerous women and newborn infants had sacrificed their lives to this necessity. Since the land was cleared and new equipment was coming along all the time to make farming easier, it seemed sensible to have fewer children to farm and to inherit the land. Miriam had witnessed what spiteful feelings her raft of siblings had about the dispensation of her father's land. Greed and jealousy had divided brothers, sisters, and the farm. Surely, with only two children, there could be peaceful division of property when the time came to hand down their acres. An increasing number of the county's children were leaving the farm entirely and going on to college, professions, and were populating Indiana's towns and cities.

It was a new day, a new generation, and a new country. Ma's Irish Catholic roots supported the custom of a baby every year, but Miriam and Ma had spoken, and Ma had confided that she thought maybe God had wanted her to stop having children earlier in her life; however, if she and Pa had chosen to be celibate for her health's sake, Miriam wouldn't have been born. The church charged couples to people the United States with many Christians. Genesis encouraged believers to "be fruitful and multiply and subdue the earth." Sexual union between a man and wife was meant for the propagation of children, not for pleasure. That was the word from the Merriam Christian Chapel pulpit. This was something she and Dave would have to think about for the future, but, as long as she was nursing the new baby, her chances of getting pregnant again were lessened. Right now, she just wanted to gaze into the eyes of this tiny, good-natured child that God had given to them.

CHAPTER 23 1889

Frank came galloping up their lane, waving his free arm, a wild look in his eyes. He called out and Miriam stuck her head out of the chicken coop to see her brother jump off his horse and run toward her. He bore dreadful news. Their brother John was dead. She put the hired woman in charge of the children, saddled Clover, and sent the hired man out to look for Dave to come with the buggy as soon as he could. Frank and Miriam rode south, their horses splashing through muddy puddles in their haste. The warm spring wind buffeted them as they rode.

Neighbors were silently milling about in John's barnyard. Miriam saw her eldest niece Florence. She dismounted and went to embrace her. What had happened? Florence, voice breaking with sobs, told her that, after breakfast, her father had said he was on his way to return Mr. Slagle's long rifle he had borrowed for hunting. He promised to hitch up the buggy and take her and Maggie to their teaching jobs as soon as he got back. A moment after he went out the back door, she heard a loud rifle blast and her father's cries. She ran and found him lying on the shed floor, dying, feet toward the door. She raised his head onto her arm. He was gasping for breath but was unconscious and could not speak to her. She saw that he had been shot on the left side and was bleeding profusely. The rifle lay on the floor on his right about three feet away. Moments later, he took his last breath and died in her arms.

Maggie rode for help and the neighbors responded. The men looked around the shed with Florence to try to figure out what had happened. He had kept the gun up on the rafter beams for safekeeping, and when he went to take it down, or when the shed door slammed shut in the wind, the gun must have fallen and discharged by accident. Florence had heard some people whispering he had committed suicide, but that just could not be true. He had no reason to take his own life. The coroner had come quickly and had ruled this tragedy an accidental death. She understood her neighbor's speculations because suicide was not unheard of in a county where life was isolated and often a difficult proposition—but not her father.

Miriam's thoughts shifted from the loss of her brother to the distraught women and boy he had left behind. She looked at the niece in her arms. The stains of her father's blood were deep crimson on her dress and arms, and she was grieving to distraction. Miriam held her closely, reassuring her that John was a fine God-fearing man who had been the innocent victim of a pure accident—a cruel twist of fate. As Miriam led Florence into the house, she saw Maggie trying to warm herself by the fireplace, but Maggie had no strength to rise from her seat on the hearth. John's wife, Ella, sat immobile in a rocking chair, drained of all emotion, staring into space. The son, Lawrence, had probably ridden to school before all this transpired. He would, no doubt, be riding in soon in a panic from the news. Ma needed to be here.

Dave had arrived in the buggy and had quickly assessed the situation. He came into the house and asked Miriam what she needed him to do first. She sent him to bear the bad tidings to Ma, to help her pack up enough clothing for several days, and to return quickly to help comfort the family and to make funeral arrangements. Miriam was sure Dave would know just how to convey this news to Ma in his calm, supportive way. What a sad state of affairs. No one had the opportunity to say goodbye to a fine man. Miriam thought about this older brother who always treated her kindly. Ma bragged on him because he was the only one of Miriam's siblings who loved school as much as she did, and he had excelled at his studies. Miriam was ashamed that she had become estranged from most of her siblings because of her defense of Brother Evan and her complete and happy adoption into the Pence clan.

John would be buried in the family plot near Pa. Ma would be so sad. It had been more than a decade since a family member had been laid to rest by the Merriam Christian Chapel—a decade blessed with new life, not death. James was forty-two, a Whitley County man all the way, and he had just reached the time of life when a fellow should be able to sit back and begin to enjoy the fruits of his labor.

Miriam thought about what it would be like to lose Dave. She didn't think she would be able to go on. She was thankful that Ella and the girls were educated women. In time, they would be able to rise out of this mournful state and continue to teach. Lawrence was bright and could finish his schooling and choose the farm or a profession as he wished. She helped Florence bathe and placed her bloody dress and undergarments into a pillowcase. Miriam would take them home and burn them. When Florence was once again dressed and had gained her composure, the two of them re-entered the living room. The four women knelt in silent prayer.

Miriam's spirits brightened as she recognized the sounds of their horse and buggy coming down the lane. Thanks be to God. Ma was here.

CHAPTER 24 1891

The children were developing their own personalities, and Miriam's hopes for the two of them to find companionship seemed to be continually dashed. Evan was five now. He had the makings of a tall man—big feet and hands—and was slender and wiry like Dave. But the resemblance ended there. Dave was thoughtful, kind, honest, and loved a good clean joke. Evan was impulsive, had a mean streak, and was learning that dishonesty got results. He loved to bully his little sister and make fun of others. He was loud and naughty around his father, and Dave was concerned. He felt that a good whipping behind the woodshed might correct some of those problems, but Miriam absolutely forbade him to lay a hand on her "sweet, silly lad." When Miriam tried to get Evan interested in his slate and letters, he would feign sleepiness. She would send him up to his room to nap, but, as soon as her back was turned, he would sneak out of the house. He was a terror in Sunday school and church. Evan had learned how to hide behind Mother's skirts when Dad came into the house bearing a rusty hand tool Evan had stolen off the bench and left out in the rain. He gained the reputation of a rapscallion during their visits to the brick house, and his girl cousins hid from him so he wouldn't pull their long hair or throw wet balls of Blue River clay onto their Sunday skirts. Dave watched his father resist the temptation to give his son a swat when Evan threw rocks at the bee hives and then sassed his grandfather, but all the family knew Miriam's ground rules for hands off Evan. Miriam and Evan were kindred spirits, and she dismissed his behavior as "boys will be boys." He most definitely was her boy.

Lilah was the total opposite of her brother. She was only three, but, from her infancy, she reserved her biggest smiles for her father. She would reach her chubby hands up to his face, stroke his sunburned forehead, and pull his prominent nose, until they would both chuckle and she would melt into his arms. When she was wakeful in her little bed upstairs, she would call "Daddy," and he, roused by her tiny voice, would climb the narrow stairs to comfort her, help her to use the chamber pot, and tuck her back in. Miriam would sometimes find them napping together in the hammock on warm afternoons—Dave's hat carefully shading Lilah's fair face. Miriam would shake her head, smile, and leave them be, like two peas in a pod. On

Sundays, Lilah could often be found standing next to Father with her hand on his knee, listening to him hold forth on some subject or another. He wore a jacket with one or two soft peppermint drops hidden just for her, and the game was to find the pocket with the treats. When Florence and her husband were not in attendance, Lilah was the youngest grandchild, and she made her rounds of everyone in the house. Her second word after "Da" was the question "Doing?" She watched with interest as the women showed her the process of shelling peas, kneading bread, cutting biscuits, and hemming skirts. Many times she was invited to help in some small way. Miriam was not as emotionally tied to Lilah, but she was gratified with her daughter. Lilah was going to be her scholar.

Miriam was intrigued by a new woman's group that had just been founded in Wolf Lake. A couple of women from church had told her about the Pythian Sisters, and, now that she had her children out of infancy, she decided it was finally time for her to make good on her promise to share her talents with the greater community. It had been eight years since she had given her solemn pledge in church, and this new society and its members intrigued her. Instead of just serving her

Christian Chapel members, the Pythian Sisters promised they honored the Bible but were not aligned with just one denomination. They claimed to not have a political affiliation, either. Miriam made up her mind to attend a meeting to see what it was all about. She would need Dave's support to take an active role in attending meetings and any other responsibilities that might come with membership, so she decided to broach the subject right away.

Buoyed by Dave's encouragement, Miriam drove the buggy into Wolf Lake to attend her first meeting of the Pythian Sisterhood. She had several friends who had attended since the first day the organization was founded and the local temple established. They were nice women, and Miriam felt she would be in good company. When Dorothy sat down to cordially invite her to come, she had asked Miriam if she had any questions. Miriam was first curious how the Pythian Sisterhood got its name. Dorothy explained that the name went back to the old days of the Greeks. Around the 4th century before Christ, Pythias and his friend Damon, both followers of the philosopher Pythagoras, traveled to Syracuse. Pythias was accused of plotting against the local tyrant and was imprisoned and sentenced to death. Pythias accepted his sentence but asked to be allowed to return home one last time, to settle his affairs and to say goodbye to his family. The tyrant refused his request. Pythias asked Damon to take his spot while he went, and the tyrant accepted the arrangement as long as, should Pythias not return one year to the day, Damon would be sacrificed instead. The day came and went and Pythias did not return. Poor Damon's head was on the chopping block, when Pythias rushed in and explained he had been attacked by pirates and had to swim to shore in order to arrive just in the nick of time. The tyrant was so impressed by the friends' trust and loyalty that he freed both men and appointed them counselors to his court. Miriam and Dorothy shared an understanding smile at such a wonderful story of friendship and loyalty.

Dorothy assured her the Pythian Sisters held these same values. They also extended their love and faithfulness to those with needs outside their membership. The men's organization, called the Fraternal Order of the Knights of Pythias, was founded in 1864 and chartered by the good President Lincoln, who wanted to find a way to ease the human conflict and suffering created by the Civil War. All the widows and orphans created by that turmoil needed assistance in order for the country to heal properly. Dorothy explained that was why the group did not have a church affiliation and was willing to help all in need, regardless of creed or politics.

That afternoon, Miriam also learned about Joseph Addison Hill, who organized the first Order of Pythian Sisters in the town of Warsaw in the county just west of Whitley County. Mr. Hill designed the symbols used in the order. His inspiration was the perfect colors of the prism seen through a raindrop. White for purity, red for love, yellow for equality, and blue for fidelity. Miriam knew immediately she had found her place among like-minded women, who would support each other and the community without fail.

Chapter 25 1896

During the next five years, Miriam was often called to attend the country doctors in the area as they delivered babies for her Pythian Sisters and those families that could not pay for a physician. The community also called upon her skills in treating horses and other livestock. She was finally doing the work God had called her to do, and it gave her great joy and satisfaction. She rode out on Clover sometimes late in the evening to tend to illness or childbirth and sometimes came back in the early light, needing rest. Her mother understood her altruism, but the Pences, even her beloved Father, began to criticize her for not concentrating her energy on her own family, especially as Evan began to skip school and continued to torment Lilah. The schoolmaster had been taking the switch to her recalcitrant son because he refused to hold his pencil in his right hand. Evan was struggling to read, as well.

For his own part, Evan figured he might as well spend his days doing what he did well: fishing, catching frogs and turtles, making forts, and using his slingshot to kill the cawing crows and flitting sparrows. It was easy to snag one of his dad's cigars from the barn where Dad had to smoke in order not to give Mother a headache. Spending a lazy day fishing was sure better than wasting all those hours in school. He didn't mind if he spent the day by himself. He could get along with himself pretty well. It was other people who set him on edge, especially that goody-goody sister of his. He needed to show her who was the boss.

One day, Evan hurled a fist-sized rock at Lilah. It struck her in the temple and knocked her out cold. Dave heard her cries and found her wobbling toward the house, Evan having fled the scene of his crime. This was the straw that broke the camel's back. Dave had restrained himself as long as he humanly could. He found Evan hiding under his bed, dragged him out of his room by his ear, turned him over his knee behind the woodshed, and gave him a sound thrashing with a cedar shingle while Miriam was gone. Evan ran to the house in tears, and Dave immediately hitched up the buggy and took Lilah to be seen by the doctor in Churubusco. When they returned, Lilah was all smiles, clutching a beautiful china doll to her chest. An intricate wicker doll buggy featuring a hanging blue parasol and big yellow wheels rocked on the floorboards by her feet. She had already named her doll Julia, and Lilah was in heaven, despite her very tender head. She gazed into Julia's delicately painted blue eyes and admired her gracefully arched brows. Her curly porcelain hair was blonde and her cheeks were tinted a rosy hue. Julia's ears were delicate, like little pale seashells, and she had on a pink dress over two layers of eyeleted petticoats. Her cloth legs ended in precious little boots with delicate silver buckles. Julia's tiny red lips were sweet, and she looked upon the world with a perpetually serene and happy expression. Her white arms were graceful, and little hands dimpled and fair. Julia was everything Lilah wished she were herself. It was fun to pretend, but Lilah knew the truth. Lilah was lanky like her father. Her teeth were crooked, so she tried to smile with her mouth shut, like Julia. She had overheard her mother unhappily comment that Lilah inherited the Waugh teeth from her father's side of the family, but there was nothing to be done about it. Lilah's hair was blonde, but thin and wispy like her mother's. She *did* share her new doll's pretty blue eyes—her best feature.

Evan, meanwhile, was sulking and nursing a sore rear end. His father had both amazed and frightened him with that spanking, but even he knew his meanness had gone over the line when he intentionally caused his sister harm. He would give that doll and buggy a wide berth; that was for sure. When Miriam saw the doctor's bandage wrapping Lilah's brow, she had to admit Dave was justified in giving Evan a whipping. Evan's reformation didn't last long, and he was back to playing the bully at school early the next week. After all, he had heard his mother say his mischief was all in fun.

The sting of Father's disapproval of her "gadding about," as he bluntly phrased it right to her face, raised Miriam's ire. She refused to go back to the brick house for Sunday dinners until she was no longer the butt of the Pences' criticism. Dave was put in an untenable position. His mother and father were leaning on him to discipline his son—and his wife. They commanded him to get his family in control so the neighbors wouldn't continue to whisper about Miriam's late night midwifery forays and Evan's naughty, dangerous behavior. He had to think of his, and the family's, reputation. Miriam knew Dave had been reproached by the Grand Patriarch, but she was not going to submit to the demands of others. Dave was going to have to choose his camp, and, until then, things would be chilly around the David M. Pence household.

Dave was gone most of one day. He

said he had business in Churubusco that would not wait, yet he refused to take Miriam and the children with him. When he returned, he drove the buggy straight toward the small storage building and disappeared inside. Miriam raised her head from her weeding of the herb garden, but, since she was finding some satisfaction in giving him the cold shoulder, she turned back to her work.

She heard Dave call her name and saw him peek around the building and beckon to her. She sighed, stood up a little stiffly, and brushed off her skirts. What could he be up to? When she walked around the building, there stood her husband and her old friend Clover. Dave stepped aside to reveal a gorgeous new side-saddle! She gasped in surprise and approached to run her hands over the buttery-soft tooled leather and the red mohair padded seat. She had never seen anything to equal its beauty and design. Her hardened heart melted as she saw Dave grinning from ear to ear. He had made his decision. She was heartened to hear him say, "Miriam, I want you to keep doing your good works, and, when you ride out on Clover, I want you to ride in safety and beauty. I want everyone to know I am so very proud of you."

He gave Miriam a leg up, and she

reveled in the comfortable seat. Dave had made detailed drawings of the stirrup length, the design, and the colors he wanted, and the saddle had been skillfully custom-made. Clover seemed to like this new saddle and its cinches, too. They both laughed as Clover shook her head and whinnied her approval. Miriam never felt so beautiful in her cotton gardening dress, circling and cantering up and down the drive to show Dave what a miracle he had wrought for her and their marriage, as well. That night, in her prayers, she chided herself for having too little faith in him. That would never happen again.

Chapter 26 1902

Buoyed by Dave's approval and her in-laws' begrudging acceptance, Miriam continued, when called upon, to ride out into the county in all seasons and hours of the day or night to assist those in need. Lilah and Evan faithfully met the horse-drawn "kid hack" at the bottom of the drive each morning of the school year. They were both well fed, dressed nicely, ears scrubbed, and books in hand. Lilah cherished her purchased schoolbooks and studied them diligently every evening. Evan was merely biding his time, trying his best to sit still in a desk until he was old enough to drop out. After Dad proved he could mete out the discipline, Evan and his father assumed a distant, cold relationship that seemed to suit them both.

When Evan reached fourteen, a boy with an unruly hank of brown hair falling over his forehead and a lean, rangy body, he finally got his wish to abandon his studies. He went to work helping Miriam and Dave on the farm, where Dad gave orders and Evan complied in order to maintain his room and board and to continue to find approval in his dear mother's eyes. His father didn't have any idea how much Evan loved this farm: the livestock, the fertile soil, every hedgerow and huckleberry bush where he had rambled and loitered as a boy. He knew this place and had no desire to live like his grandparents had—pushing into new territory and working to exhaustion on the land to scrape out a living. No one with any sense did that any more. He knew young single men who farmed, but still had time to head into Churubusco for evenings at the saloon with drinks and cigars and to hang around with the fellows at the livery stable and the barber shop. A bachelor farmer life sounded good to him, and he would take care of his mother as long as she lived, no matter what. That's what his old uncle had done, until late in life Uncle Evan had finally married the hired girl. They had a baby boy now, but he and his wife still lived on the home place and took care of Ma Coulter.

Evan had his mother's flashing eyes, her impatience, and her quick temper that he often turned toward his sister in frustration. He had prayed to God for a brother, but, instead, got a sister who would rather read books and play inside with her stupid china doll than climb trees and fish with him. The teachers all fawned over her, and his father thought she could do no wrong. She was pathetic, and the fewer dealings he had with her, the better.

When she was thirteen, Lilah enrolled in the big, two story high school in Churubusco. Miriam was thrilled her daughter was interested in continuing her schooling, and she had dreams of her attending Valparaiso University, following in the footsteps of her Aunt Florence. Miriam arranged for Lilah to board during the school week with Coulter cousins who had moved to town and had a room to let. Perhaps Lilah could find herself a lawyer to marry, too, and rise up in the social circles of Columbia City, Indianapolis, or even Chicago. A modern American woman could have everything. Lilah could live a life of comfort with a beautiful home and coveted memberships in the Daughters of the American Revolution, literary clubs, and a big church and its women's circles.

Lilah's high school teachers praised her potential and encouraged her to become a teacher. They all told her they would be proud to have her in their profession. She took that praise seriously with lowered eyes and a blush at the compliment, but, within weeks of her high school matriculation, she experienced a definite distraction to her studies from an unlikely source. Her attention strayed because of the star athlete in high school. His name was George McConnell, and he was a dashing boy. She had known him all her life because he and his family came to Sunday school and church at the Merriam Christian Chapel, but she hadn't had much interest in boys during her young life—and he seemed quiet and reserved around the others. She had heard that he came from a rich family. He rode double into Churubusco on Sunday nights behind his brother Ike, and the two boys "batched it," doing their own cooking, getting to school under their own volition during the week, and going to their team practices and high school games for fun. They always rode back to the farm on Friday night to help with the weekend chores.

When she was a freshman, he was a senior, and she couldn't believe he had eyes for her, but he smiled her way whenever they met in the hallways. One day he called her away from her group of girlfriends, spoke to her for the first time, and invited her to stop by the diamond after school and watch him pitch a home game. She had never seen a real baseball game before; she had never paid attention when Evan ran off to play in the churchyard with the other boys. Lilah didn't even know the rules of the game, but she asked one of her local girlfriends to go along, too. The two girls heard the game from a distance, long before they saw it. A loud, enthusiastic local crowd of all ages filled the rickety bleachers; on a little elevated mound of clay dirt, in the center of attention, was George.

George leaned forward at the waist and intently studied the catcher's signals, his dark brown mitt resting on his thigh. He wore a dusty, loose-fitting uniform and a tight cap with a short brim. Lilah could see, under his cap, his hair was parted in the middle and slicked back. Long dark socks met his pants at the knees and she could see spiked cleats on his shoe soles. People in the crowd chanted his name. He was a handsome boy with a strong jaw and piercing eyes. His frame was lean; his short sleeves revealed muscular forearms. His large right hand enveloped the baseball.

Lilah realized she had never really gotten a good look at George before. Why did she feel compelled to lower her eyes and act so demure when he spoke to her at school? Her mother sure wouldn't act like that. Mother wanted her to be confident, but the more Mother pushed her, the more self-conscious she became. To be honest, it was sort of nice to be out of Mother's sight during the week, and, she had to admit, though she missed her Dad, she shouldn't allow him to baby her anymore. She was thirteen, and it was good to be alive. The bleachers shook as the crowd rose to its feet and called out, "Mac, Mac, Mac, Mac!"

Lilah was caught up in the thrill of the game and raised her voice in the chant.

She watched the batters struggling to hit George's powerful pitches. "One strike...two, three...you're out!" the umpire cried. The men laughed, slapped dusty hats on each other's shoulders, and reveled in the Eagles' victory. As George loped to the little makeshift dugout, he caught Lilah's eye and smiled a big toothy grin. She grinned back, looking right at him, keeping her lips carefully closed, of course. But her eyes crinkled at the corners, and the normally so-serious girl was transformed at that moment. Good. She had held his handsome gaze and hadn't died on the spot.

Encouraged by Lilah's smile, George decided to court this demure gal. His parents would approve of her, he knew. The McConnells worshipped in the same church with her family. His mother admired Mrs. Pence's midwifery and good works, and his father was impressed with Mr. Pence's progressive farm and healthy livestock. Plus, George liked quiet girls. The giggly, pushy ones were too demanding. He liked to play hard but take life a little easy. He would be darned if he would get up before dawn to milk cows and slop hogs when *he* had a farm. He could work as hard as any man, but the work had to fit into a reasonable schedule to leave time for playing baseball, horseshoes, billiards, and basketball. Any girl of his would have to like to sleep in, be his helpmate to get things done, and then be willing to either let him go play or, better yet, come to watch him from the sidelines. He could even teach a gal to play, if she was a sport. That's what he needed—a sport.

Lilah proved to be the one. She came to his games, clapped and cheered for him and the team, and then let him walk her back hand-in-hand to her cousin's house. She went to the school dances and parties with him his senior year. She had an easy laugh, was incredibly kind and thoughtful, and was a graceful dancer. She and her cousin fried a chicken or baked a pie for the two brothers once in a while to take to their bachelor quarters and to devour with two forks straight out of the pan. George and Lilah proved to be a handsome couple on the dance floor; he was six feet tall and she was only a few inches shorter. They did a little spooning in the parlor of her cousin's house, as much as was possible with family in and out, but she refused to go with him to his boarding house alone. He acted put out, but secretly he was glad she was an upstanding girl, unlike some of the others he knew who did not guard their reputations carefully.

George graduated and immediately

went to work for Ike, who had just established a contractor business. That was the way homes were built these days; house-raisings had gone by the wayside. That was old-timey pioneer stuff. No one wanted a little log house anymore. Most of them had been abandoned and were growing up in weeds or put to use as tool storage or housing for seasonal help. He was excited to follow the carpenter trade. It fit his lifestyle and he was good at it. Pounding nails, setting shingles, climbing around on the open framing like a monkey, even doing the finish work on cabinetry interested him and kept him in good physical shape. He was saving money, too. He didn't have to report for work until after the sun was up and he had a good breakfast, and Ike promised him he could juggle his hours so he could still play baseball with the men's team. Oh, how he wished he could make it to the big league as a pitcher. Cy Young was pitching up a storm, and he loved following the Chicago White Sox. They usually came in pretty high in the American League. He really enjoyed hanging around with the Churubusco fellows, though, and he got some glory for being a local sports hero. Everyone had a smile and a pat on the back for him, and the men hanging around the barber shop listened to his every word. Mr.

Young gave him free cigars handmade from Whitley County tobacco. Despite his celebrity, he was living back on the farm with his folks like a kid, and that had to change now he was twenty-one. His dear Lilah would be part of that change.

As their courting continued and he became sure of Lila's friendship, affection, and then love, he took her to visit the farm to spend time with his parents and Grandmother McConnell who lived with them and had played a great part in his moral upbringing. He got to know Mr. and Mrs. Pence pretty well, too. They seemed to like him, though they weren't as impressed with his baseball skills as most people in the county, and Mrs. Pence got a disappointed look in her eye when he told her he was saving to buy a farm. He guessed he had said something wrong, but he was darned if he could figure out what it was. He admired their neat, productive farm, and Mr. Pence had invited him to walk out into the fields and take a look at his Angus cows; he was sure proud of those black, shiny beauties. From watching the happy homecoming embraces between father and daughter, George could tell he was going to have to win over Lilah's father, if he was to have a chance to ask for her hand in marriage one of these days—and that was what he had in mind.

Lilah's brother Evan was a good fellow. He had played church baseball with him for years. Evan just liked to have a good time and got carried away once in a while, but they were only two years apart in age and considered each other friends. It didn't take long to figure out that Lilah and her brother were not close. They seemed to avoid each other at all costs. He would probably need to ask Lilah about that some day, but for now, as his father would say, leave sleeping dogs lie.

He even overcame a severe case of the nerves and accompanied Lilah to meet her grandparents in the big house for Sunday dinner. That was a stressful experience, with the old man sporting that long white beard and passing judgment on him. He guessed he did all right, and his knees didn't knock too much. To his surprise, he discovered JJ Pence followed box scores in the paper and liked to play horseshoes, and that gave them some common ground. He sure was on his best behavior, and the old man shook his hand warmly when they climbed into the buggy to leave. Lilah's Grandma Coulter was getting old, too. She asked him to call her Ma, and so he did. She wasn't real well, but Lilah's Uncle Evan and his young wife were giving her good care in their big old house where the peacocks reigned in the yard.

Lilah laughed when the biggest male, running at full speed, was a match for George the first time they visited her farm. He sprinted across the lawn with the beautiful, iridescent, aggressive bird, streaming its long colorful tail, hot on his heels! After he had outrun the blasted thing, he carefully peered around the corner of the woodshed and saw Lilah doubled over with laughter. It was quite a sight and made for great entertainment for Ma as she stood in the doorway waiting to be introduced to her granddaughter's fleet-footed beau who could outrun the rainbow.

Miriam still held out high hopes for her daughter, who was swiftly coming to a crossroads in her life. Miriam found it hard to talk to Lilah as she turned sixteen. There were so many things for her to know about becoming a woman, but, even though Miriam could be frank and forthcoming with all the neighbor women she counseled in pregnancy and child care, she found it difficult to talk to her own daughter about these delicate subjects and the responsibilities of marriage. Her daughter was an accomplished seamstress, but her cooking repertoire consisted of apple and cream pies. Dave was no help. He adored his daughter so much he lost all perspective when it came to giving her guidance. He could not accept his little girl was growing up and would be making adult decisions about her life. Would Lilah choose college and a career, or would she marry the McConnell boy and be a farmwife? She had already been accepted into Valparaiso University for the fall to study to become a teacher, and Miriam was determined Lilah should continue her education and become an accomplished 20th century woman.

Miriam's worries were in vain. The

glowing young couple arrived unexpectedly in the drive. Without the benefit of their parents' collective wisdom, Lilah and George had made their own decision. Lilah ran to her father and gave him a hug. She showed him a pretty ruby and onyx ring on the third finger of her left hand. Yes, it was true. She and George were to be married in one year. During their betrothal, she would attend two semesters at "Valpo," and George would figure out where they would live. In the spring, she was going to leave her studies and become Mrs. George McConnell. She would be seventeen by then, and George twenty-one. Miriam managed a smile at the couple, and then she turned and walked toward the house so no one would see her tears.

Chapter 28 1905

The betrothal supper was going to be a festive event at the McConnell farm, and Miriam and Dave donned their best clothing for the event. They were still getting used to the idea of their young daughter's engagement and were uneasy about the whole thing. What did the McConnells think of this impending union? Although they went to the same church, they knew little about this family of relative newcomers to Whitley County. William McConnell and his wife Louisa arrived from Ohio when George was a small child and bought 200 acres in Smith Township, near Round Lake. They built a beautiful, big frame house and planted fruit trees and extensive gardens—that much the Pences could see from driving past. They had never been inside the house, though.

Dave and Miriam rode in the front seat of the buggy; a reluctant Evan slouched next to Ma in the back. As they trotted up the McConnell lane, they saw a crowd of people out on the large front lawn. A spirited game of croquet was in session. The ladies wore their pretty summer dresses and the men were in their shirtsleeves. A gaggle of white geese honked a warning to the family, and everyone paused from their playing to welcome the visitors, waving hands and raising mallets. What a beautiful sight. Lilah and George were lounging side by side in a fringed hammock suspended between two hickory trees. They hopped up, hurried over, helped Ma from the buggy, and seated her in a comfortable wicker chair on the lawn overlooking the game. Ma's eyes crinkled and she was all smiles. She already liked this clan who knew how to have some fun.

William McConnell greeted Dave with a hearty handshake and made a gentlemanly bow to Miriam. Lilah took Miriam's arm, and she and George took her in to meet Louisa, who was busy in the kitchen, as usual. William invited Dave to take a look around the place, and Dave was delighted. It was a lovely farm. The family had planted every kind of fruit tree and berry bush, and the profuse gardens were yielding all the summer crops. Lush plants with deep green leaves wound up poles and already were heavily hung with long string beans. Vines crept around the bottoms of the poles, and their beautiful orange blooms promised a good supply of winter squash in the root cellar by fall's harvest. Rows of bell peppers, carrots, beets, and potatoes had all been painstakingly thinned and weeded. The borders of the garden featured orange marigolds and creamy yellow nasturtiums in full bloom. Chickens and guinea hens scattered about the men's feet, and turkeys strutted in the barnyard. Dave looked with envy at the large bank barn. He just about had enough saved to build his own. William's barn housed implements and two doe-eyed Guernsey milk cows lowing in a stall. A team of fine workhorses whinnied a greeting, and Dave could hear squealing of little pigs and the soft snuffling and grunting of the hogs in the pen outside. His father would sure like to see this place, and he was glad Father and Alice were on the way to supper, too. Lilah would find great financial security within this family; he was convinced of it. That was a great comfort, and he found himself relaxing in the presence of this affable man. Dave produced a couple of locally-made cigars, and they lighted them in an informal ritual of solidarity—one man of the soil to another. The marriage of the children would be the unification of two good families, and all would be well.

Miriam marveled at the two story house with elaborate wood turnings and gingerbread decoration on the porch, and she smiled with delight when she was ushered into the parlor. Louisa had furnished it in the latest style with substantial things: a full-size rug with red rose design, an upright piano on one wall, and a pretty humpback sofa with two matching chairs. There were lovely framed pictures. In a prominent place hung a portrait of Christ surrounded by children: "Suffer the little children to come unto Me," Miriam whispered to herself. It was one of Ma's favorite verses, and she would be glad to see it, too.

Sitting in a corner rocking chair was a beautiful elderly woman. Lilah introduced her as Grandmother McConnell, who had come with the family from Ohio. She had tended to the children while Louisa worked side by side with her husband to create this beautiful farm and, in turn, to afford all these wonderful things. George had told Miriam his grandmother had given him and his brothers and sisters daily Bible lessons, without fail. She was a Presbyterian and strong in her faith. He could recite whole chapters of verse due to her teaching, and he gave her credit for much of the good that could be found in him. The two touched hands gently in greeting, and the elderly women softly said, "Please, call me Mary."

Lilah ushered her mother through the dining room next. Their feet sank into soft wall-to-wall Brussels carpet. The large table was surrounded by a matching set of oak chairs with tall backs and brown leather seats. The table was set for twelve with beautiful matching china plates, crystal, and silver. A carbide gas chandelier hung over the table, crystal prisms suspended from the perimeter like icicles. The linen tablecloth and initialed napkins were exquisite. A heavy oak china cabinet sat along one wall, and the adjoining wall featured a matching sideboard for the linens. An elegant silver tea set and two matching green vases graced the sideboard. Miriam had never seen such a beautiful color of glass. Lilah was going to be well cared for as a member of this family of means.

Miriam began to enjoy her tour even more. George ushered her into the living room and, just for fun, seated her in his father's Morris chair. It had flat oak arms and an upholstered seat and back. George punched a button on the arm, and Miriam found her feet and legs flying up and her head reclining. She ended up staring at the ceiling in amazement. She had never seen such a thing as a chair that featured a clever built-in footstool, but she believed it would be comfortable enough to sleep in. A large library table with shelves at each end for books and magazines had been placed under one window, and the room had a black leather couch long enough to stretch out for an afternoon nap. One of the hand-stitched pillows was black satin with a white cat embroidered on it—beautiful, highly accomplished work. A brand new Victor record player, complete with a hand crank and big horn, was sitting on a square oak table. Miriam had seen a player like this for sale in Columbia City but had never heard one play. She hoped music was on the program for the evening. Lace curtains framed every window and wafted gently in the breeze. The sounds of the croquet game came in through the windows, and Miriam was especially gratified to hear her son's laughter.

The clatter of pots and pans led them into the kitchen. Pretty, plump Louisa McConnell looked up from the cast iron wood stove. Her brown hair was pinned in a bun on the top of her head. Her face was kind and her brown eyes sparkled. Her cheeks were flushed from the heat rising off the stove, and she put down her wooden spoon and greeted Miriam with a hug. She wore a kitchen apron with red bric-a-brac to protect a white dress with a light blue lace collar and mother-of-pearl buttons. Louisa invited Miriam to sit down at the round kitchen table and sent Lilah into the pantry to bring three cool glasses of lemonade from the pottery crock. Miriam was amazed that this little woman did all the work on this big house with no hired help. Their oldest child, Bertha, lived across the road with her husband, Volnie. Ike and George were good help for their father. Mary and Ross were still at home and everyone, it seemed, pitched in to help with the house and farm. This family seemed so close and cheerful, and Miriam saw how Lilah had come to feel very much at home here.

Lilah had told her that the McConnells never hired anything done. If the house needed painting, the parlor needed new wallpaper, or there were carpentry jobs to be done, the family answered the call. They harvested all their crops as a team. They gathered together the week after Christmas to butcher the hogs and divided the meat among them. In the dead of winter, the family all gathered to harvest blocks of ice from Round Lake. George used an auger to drill an initial hole in the foot-thick, clear ice, and the men took turns wielding an ice saw to create one foot square blocks. This outing always culminated in skating races between the boys, and they watched in awe and cheered as their father performed his annual figure eights. Mulled cider and ginger cookies kept them warm and fed during this day that was hard work, but mostly fun. The blocks were hauled back to the farm, stacked in the partially-underground icehouse with lots of sawdust under and around them. Ross's job was to place a new block into his mother's oak icebox about twice a week. The melted water drained out a hole in the kitchen wall and watered a rambler rose bush. He also happily chipped it into little chunks for the ice cream churn every 4th of July.

Miriam observed first-hand what a loving family could accomplish, and it made her mournful that her brothers and sisters were acting more and more contentious toward one another as their mother grew older. The McConnells had found a much better way to get along, and Miriam sadly wondered what Pa would think to see his children at each other's throats over the dispensation of his few acres of land. The sounds from the croquet game spoke volumes for this family; the laughter after each sharp click of the balls was infectious. The family was having so much fun together and had included Ma and Evan in their sport. She realized where George had learned his love of games, good competition, and teamwork. Maybe marrying a baseball player wasn't such a bad thing, after all, if it brought this sort of joy to life.

Meanwhile, William was in the cellar giving Dave a tutorial on the most modern convenience of all. He had recently invested in carbide lighting for his home, and he had been itching to show someone how it worked. A salesman had been by and sang the praises of the Monarch Acetylene Gas Lighting Generator, and there it sat in its glory before them. They both laughed when Dave said if he didn't know better he would think it was a whiskey still. Running from this machine, composed of stacked metal boxes and a tank, was a small pipe. The metal pipe ran up the wall and disappeared through the ceiling. William showed Dave how every four weeks he merely had to pour a sack of carbide pellets in the hopper. The pellets fed automatically down into a tank of water and formed acetylene gas, which filled the tank and the copper pipes running to his lighting fixtures on the main floor. All a body had to do to get a nice white light was to turn a little knob on the fixture and light the mantle with a match. The smell and danger of kerosene or coal oil lamps was gone from the downstairs, and he figured to run gas up to the bedrooms when he got a chance. Reflectors behind the glowing mantles threw out light plenty good enough to read by, and his Louisa was mighty tickled with the dining room chandelier he had bought her last Christmas. It sure brightened up the winters to have good lighting in the house. He would recommend this modern system to Dave for his own home until the time came when electric lines would be strung all the way out to Smith Township. He smiled and told Dave, when that happened, his sweet Louisa would be the first to have an electric stove and indoor plumbing. Imagine that.

As Dave climbed out of the cellar, he reflected on his growing admiration for William, who seemed to have the best of everything. He was a real go-getter, and Dave was glad to know him better. No wonder he had raised a fine son. George came from good stock.

CHAPTER 29 1906

According to plan, in the fall, Lilah packed her bags, bade a tearful farewell to George, and took the train to Valparaiso to begin a year of teacher training. There was a little cottage close by Miriam and Dave's farm, and the young couple would move there after the wedding until a suitable farm could be located for them. The two families furnished the cottage nicely in stylish golden oak furniture, and it promised to be a snug home. George helped on both parents' farms that fall, lived at home, played ball, and pined for Lilah. He held his breath until the Thanksgiving holiday when he met her at the train station and whisked her off in the buggy to spend some time alone. On several occasions, his two employers took pity on the lovesick, lonely boy and allowed him a long weekend to pay Lilah a visit at school. He loved those trips because he and Lilah took the train into Chicago for the day. They walked the lakeshore and spent a good deal of George's cash for a good lunch. The violent Teamster's Strike was over, but the crush of the city put George's nerves on edge. They rode electric trolley cars down the dusty city streets and loved to stand and watch the toll bridges slowly open to let the tugboats and ships through into Lake Michigan. He always had to get Lilah back to student housing by curfew, though. George was counting the days until they could be together. Absence had made both hearts grow fonder.

Lilah wore an ivory gown on the day she exchanged wedding vows with George. She was slender and poised, and her hair was soft around her face and gathered in the back in the latest style. As they took their vows in the Christian Chapel that had been their church home since they had been children, they felt the warmth and comfort of family all about them. The Coulters came to show their respect for Miriam and were tolerant of each other for the day, to Ma's great relief. The McConnells came in droves; even some of their Ohio relatives made the trip, and their happy faces lent a festive air to the proceedings. Until the last vow was spoken, Miriam still held mixed feelings about this union. She looked over at Louisa, who was dabbing her eyes with a lacy handkerchief. William was patting her on the back. Dave's eyes were welling, but Miriam could not cry.

After the service, Miriam took Ma's arm, and they walked through the cemetery to visit Pa's graveside. Ma's breathing was labored from the walk, and she steadied herself with one hand on Pa's stone. Miriam looked closely at her mother. Her familiar "laugh lines" had become deep wrinkles. Her hair was white and her skin pale. She was stooped and her dress hung on her. Miriam feared it would not be long until Ma joined Pa in this place, but the cemetery was cool and lovely, and, from her silence, Miriam knew Ma was lost in her memories. They rested there until Dave drove the buggy close.

Chapter 30   1907

During their first months of marriage, Lilah and George found out how wonderfully compatible they were. Their little house was cozy, and they relished George's one day off when they would sleep late; do their chores before breakfast; cook oatmeal, toast, bacon and eggs side by side; and linger over their coffee. They would plan their day, which might include a buggy ride to Churubusco, some shopping, an ice cream sundae, and a late afternoon baseball game. George had gotten to be a fair to middling cook during his bachelor days, and his mother made sure all her children, including the boys, had basic skills. Lilah had been learning in Louisa's cheerful, sunshine-filled kitchen, too. She went to the McConnells on the days George worked there, and her patient, kind mother-in-law taught her how to make jams and jellies and how to safely preserve meats and vegetables. Lilah helped in the gardens with joy. She learned from Louisa how to cut George's hair the way he liked it, and sometimes he would get out the shaving basin and relax as she lathered his face and skillfully shaved him with his straight razor—nary a cut. She enjoyed laying out his clean and mended work clothes over the back of the bedroom chair each night to save him time in the mornings. She was happy doing little things for her handsome, kind husband, and he often took time to pick flowers for the table, presenting them to her with a flourish and a warm embrace. He would pick his teenage bride off the floor in his strong arms and swing her around and around.

Within months of their wedding, Lilah was pregnant. She did not go to her own mother with the news, though. She and George first told Louisa. Miriam was deeply hurt by her daughter's slight. This was going to be her first grandchild. Louisa already had many grandchildren, and Miriam felt she should have the right to first spread the word throughout the neighborhood. She held a grudge and was disgruntled at Dave, who was immediately ecstatic at the news and was showering gifts on his daughter. He bought blocks, rattles, and a stuffed lamb. Lilah came home one day to find a petite twig rocking chair installed by her hearth. In April, her father had let the gypsy artisan and his family camp on his property by the river, and the man had performed his magic with willow. The chair was perfect. Its flexible honey-colored branches cradled her in comfort, and Lilah sat back and dreamed of nursing her baby before the glowing embers of the fire. She and George were so excited to start their family. George was hoping for a boy. He would teach young Georgie to throw a baseball and catch fish and lightning bugs.

Lilah had been very uncomfortable all spring. The baby wasn't due until late June. She finally turned to her mother's expertise in pregnancy and childbirth, and Miriam felt included in her daughter's life, once again. George insisted on making arrangements with a new young general practitioner in Churubusco. The doctor was ready to report to the house when summoned. It was going to be Dave's job to get word to the doctor and to lead him back post-haste.

Lilah was in a weakened condition from her sedentary winter and spring when her labor pains began, and the baby was slow to be born. George was beside himself with worry. Dave was no help. After seeing to the doctor's arrival, Dave was frantically pacing, too, and finally excused himself to the barnyard, where George saw him wrapped in a plume of cigar smoke, standing stock-still. Dave was staring at the side of the barn, seemingly contemplating everything and nothing. Lilah's sobs, followed by a baby's weak cries finally emanated from the bedroom. The doctor emerged, looking spent. Miriam followed, hands clenched, her eyes flashing in anger. She told George in a loud whisper the doctor he had hired was an incompetent quack, and his carelessness had nearly cost Lilah's life during the delivery. Dave was put in charge of getting the doctor paid, mollified after the tongue lashing, and chased off the place while George went in to meet his baby daughter, Helen. He and Lilah had decided on that name, if the baby was a girl, because they both fondly remembered their study of Homer's *Iliad*. Helen was the most beautiful mortal, and she was famous for the "face that launched a thousand ships." Her legend had miraculously found its way from ancient Greece all the way into the brick schoolhouses of small town Indiana.

George's first concern was for Lilah, his best friend. He was so sorry she had to suffer so to bring this child into the world. Her face was pale against the pillowcase. She was asleep and breathing softly. George knelt by the bed and kissed her gently on her cheek, still flushed and mottled from her exertion. She stirred but didn't awaken. He had often heard the mourning doves in the dawn, turned in bed, and memorized Lilah's sleeping face before dozing off again, so he could tell she was going to be all right by her untroubled brow and soft respiration. She looked like an angel. Miriam had entered the room and was standing with a bundle in her arms. He peeked into the swaddling clothes and a little round face peered out, blinking at him. So this was the one who had caused so much pain and commotion. Miriam offered Dave the bundle, but he waved her off and turned back to stroke Lilah's hand and wrist.

Now that her daughter was out of danger, Miriam held this child in her arms in wonder. A grandchild. This tiny girl was perfect. She had counted all the fingers and toes when she had given Helen her first sponge bath with nice warm water. For an infant who had come through a traumatic delivery, she was in good condition. She was breathing well, and her little arms and legs kicked and jerked normally during the bath. She laid the swaddled baby in her cradle, and Helen drifted off into a sound sleep without a peep.

Miriam knew Lilah needed rest after her ordeal. She was still angry about the botched delivery and concerned about her daughter's ability to bear more children. The doctor's clumsy use of forceps had caused uncommon bleeding and perhaps permanent scarring of the uterus. For many anxious moments during her labor, Lilah's pulse had remained dangerously weak. Miriam would employ all her nursing skills to help Lilah regain her strength. She was glad the summer was here. There would be lots of opportunity for Lilah to get the sunshine and exercise she would need to carry on her responsibilities as wife and mother. The McConnells were negotiating on a farm in Thorncreek Township for George and Lilah, so she would need to spend time getting well acquainted with the new baby while they were still in the neighborhood.

CHAPTER 31 1908

Evan's late-in-life marriage to the sweet seventeen year old hired girl Sal was an embarrassment to his brothers, but Miriam had helped to deliver two boys and a girl to the couple on the old homestead. The place rang with the music of small children once more, and the coat rack was filled with a colorful array of little hats, coats, and scarves. Evan and Sal were still caring for Ma, whose steps and memory were faltering more and more each Sunday—until one Sunday when their buggy did not arrive at church at all. After the service, Miriam asked Dave to drive her by Ma's place, and, as they came up the long lane, it was obvious there was trouble at the house. Evan was on the front steps with his head in his hands. Sal was seated beside him, arm around his shoulders. Ma was dead. She had passed away in her sleep the night before.

Miriam gazed upon her mother's still body. The deep creases of her "laugh lines" were softened in death, and she looked at peace with the world. Sal had found her favorite green dress Ma had sewn for Miriam's wedding and, after washing her body carefully, had dressed her in her finest, put on her gold necklace, and brushed her hair. Sal and Evan had placed her body lovingly on the bed, hands crossed over a bouquet of her favorite tiger lilies until the family could be summoned to make arrangements.

Coulters began to roll in as the news spread, and, by afternoon, the clan had all assembled. A shaky truce was established in respect for Ma, and it was quiet at the old farmhouse that held so many memories for each of them. Dave took the buggy and went to get George. Lilah was still not able to travel, but Dave and George would go into Churubusco and buy a ready-made casket. The preacher arrived, led the family in a prayer that was heavy into pointed words of reconciliation and love, and they set the funeral for two days later. Ma would like an Irish wake, they all decided. Visitation would be in the rainbow room decorated with flowers, and the cut glass vase of peacock feathers would have a prominent place by the coffin. Two of them would sit with the body at all times until Ma would take her rightful place next to Pa. Miriam was comforted by the thought the two of them would finally be together in Heaven, with Willie and the other darling babies, all happy and well.

Evan loudly ended the truce at the family meal after the funeral, however, by announcing he was leaving the farm. He and Sal were taking the contents of the house and moving to Columbia City. He was finished with all the bickering and wanted to be shut of his Coulter relatives, other than Miriam, who had managed to be distant, but kind. Miriam hated to witness the outrage at Evan's announcement, but she had predicted a conflict that would probably outlast them all. Each of her brothers and her sister made haste to his or her lawyer, and litigation ensued. She had feared that outcome, and it had come to pass even before the grass could grow over their mother's grave.

Chapter 32   1910

Dave and Miriam were hitching up the bay mare to take a buggy ride over to see George, Lilah, and the baby, when they heard ungodly noises coming up the drive. The horse reared up in fright, eyes rolling and ears back, as a brand new Maxwell touring car came to a halt by the side of the house. William McConnell hopped out, dressed to the nines in a driving cap, goggles, and a long duster coat that reached clear to his ankles. The young bay continued to be spooked by this strange apparition, and Miriam had to speak to her sharply to settle her down. The machine was still chugging and spewing foul-smelling exhaust fumes, but finally sputtered to a halt. William was beaming from ear to ear, and she and Dave could only stand with their mouths open in surprise when Louisa hopped down out of the passenger seat dressed in a flowing scarf, goggles, and her own tan duster. Her short, stocky stature was accentuated by the odd costume, and Miriam and Dave finally came back to their senses enough to look at one another and then break out in a gale of laughter, joined by the good-natured McConnells. In the back seat were none other than George, Lilah, and baby Helen enjoying a ride in the horseless carriage— the first one ever purchased to be driven on the dusty roads of Smith Township. Dave and Miriam had seen a growing number of automobiles in Columbia City before, but none way out here where the roads were still mostly dirt. Only a few improved roads in the county were topped with coarse gravel. What would William think of next? Dave marveled at the man.

William was giving rides, so Miriam and Dave took their first spin in an automobile that day. It was thrilling to feel the wind in their faces and listen to the engine roar. Afterward, Miriam could see the gleam in Dave's eyes as William showed him the engine compartment and the spoked wheels and rubber tires. Miriam looked wistfully at the elderly, retired Clover, eyeing them from the pasture gate. Would horses be deemed useless in the future? This country was settled by horsepower. She thought of the beautiful Normans her brother had sold to pull canal boats up and down the Wabash Canal. She thought of the horses that had given their lives to turn the soil and pull the buggies and the big covered wagons. Perhaps their time had passed. Flying machines were coming on fast, too. Could you imagine that? Her children and grandchildren would be able to fly through the air and look down on the farms and towns below. She thought her heart would burst if she were forced to ride in an airplane. Flying down the road in this automobile was enough of a thrill for her.

Miriam's reverie was broken when Louisa told her that her boy Ross disliked farming, but he had fallen in love with motorcars. He and his father had been lured by the advertising claiming the cost per passenger mile in the Maxwell was just slightly more than one cent, as opposed to two and a half cents for driving a horse and buggy. Ross argued the Maxwell wasn't an extravagance. He claimed owning an automobile would actually be a savings of money and time. Louisa chuckled at that. William bought it on Ross's urging, with the stipulation that Ross was to maintain the machine and make sure it was always in running order, shiny, and ready to go at a moment's notice. Ross and William had taken the train to Fort Wayne to buy this new contraption. If she ever wanted to find Ross these days, he had his head in the engine compartment or was lying underneath the Maxwell, fiddling with belts and such. He was the only one of them who knew what made it go.

The next Sunday, the McConnells arrived at church for the first time in their new horseless carriage. William and Ross were sitting in front, and Mary and Louisa were in the back seat. All four of them were in their driving costumes and made quite an impression on the men visiting outside before the service. Most of the fellows had to scramble to settle their scared horses. When William saw the commotion he was causing, he cranked the steering wheel as hard as he could and parked clear on the other side of the church. Everyone flinched as the auto backfired and sputtered to a stop. The McConnells had experienced a bumpy ride, and the two ladies looked flustered as they made their way to the church—all eyes on them and their machine of the future. It stood there on those four big wheels—so obedient, so shiny. Everyone wondered if the fad could possibly catch on.

CHAPTER 33 1911

Dave had saved religiously for years. The good return from his well-fed cattle allowed him to go ahead with the building of his barn. He had long dreamed of a place to house his own implements, his eight horses, the milk cows, pigs, sheep, and hay and grain for the animals. The new barn was watched over by the family cats that killed the mice and rats. Miriam despised the cats that tormented her chickens, but Dave reminded her, "Cats pay for their keep." The implement shed still housed the hand tools, wagon, and the buggy—maybe an automobile before too long, if he could just convince Miriam. The majestic windmill next to the barn continued to pump cool, fresh water for the gardens and the animals.

The barn's skeleton was constructed of massive hewn oak posts and beams, tenoned into one another and pegged. Handling the big timbers had required the help of Ike's crew, who were skilled in framing with block and tackle. The barn was covered with clapboard siding to match the house, and George and Evan did the painting, using gallons upon gallons of white barn paint. As the finishing touch,

Dave set up his tallest ladder, climbed to the top with a quart of black enamel, a one inch brush, and a clean rag in his pocket. With a steady hand, he carefully painted "19 David M. Pence 11" in large block letters above the sliding barn doors. From his elevated position, he was king of all he surveyed. He looked back at the house and saw Miriam, arms crossed, smiling up at him with satisfaction. My, how he loved that woman. She could be difficult, independent to a fault, outspoken, and quick tempered, but they had been a perfect fit all these years. She knew what this crowning moment meant to him. He was a man of means, a progressive farmer from the great State of Indiana. He could climb down off this ladder, but this feeling of being on top of the world would stay with him forever.

Chapter 34   1916

Evan never believed any woman could compare with his mother Miriam until, one day in town, he met sweet Bess, who seemed to adore him just the way he was. He had finally found a woman who shared his love of the outdoors and having fun, and she didn't mind if he had a drink with the fellows when Dad would give him a day off. She liked to fish, to garden, and didn't seem to mind picking up after him. She had lured him in with her cooking; after his first forkful of her succulent, spicy apple pie, he was smitten. Before their marriage, Bess had anxiously told him the doctors had pronounced her unable to bear children. She shed happy tears when he hugged her and said that was fine with him; he liked youngsters like his niece Helen, but he had no desire to have the responsibility or cost of raising his own. They had married quietly in her church with just a small contingency of family in attendance.

George, Lilah, and Helen had moved onto their own farm in Long Swamp in Thorncreek Township, so he and Bess moved into the little cottage they had left behind. He still worked for Dad, and, as long as Mother smoothed things over between the two of them, the work suited him fine. Bess was a peacemaker, as well, and Dad seemed to like her because he discovered she could read, write, and cipher real well. Bess had also quietly suggested to him that he needed to try to get along with his father, if they were going to have any hope of inheriting the farm. Bess wholeheartedly agreed with him that his sister Lilah was vain and proud, and his wife's loyalty to his opinions gave Evan a great deal of satisfaction. His mother was cold toward Bess, but she seemed relieved he had someone capable to care for him, instead of ending up alone in this life.

Lilah was enjoying decorating her own pretty two story frame house. She planted lots of flowers in the yard and placed pots of scarlet geraniums all along the front porch railing, just as her mother had done for years. George was a willing helper in all projects, and, after nine years of her mother's good nursing advice, her health had greatly improved. She unexpectedly found herself pregnant again, which pleased the whole family. George's land had a lot of acres of fertile, sandy soil reclaimed from the nearby swamp that were not suitable for corn, but he was convinced he could do something profitable with the black northern Indiana muck. He knew there was an increasing demand for peppermint oil. Charles Wrigley, a fellow baseball lover, had given up selling soap and baking powder in Chicago and was concentrating on the production of chewing gum. George had heard from a drummer that mucky soil was perfect for peppermint, so he signed a contract with Mr. Wrigley, planted his first starts, and watched them send out their dark-green runners in all directions. His neighbors thought he was foolish to take such a risk with an untried crop, but he persevered, though he knew they were whispering about him in Churubusco. Mint growing required a constant fight against any weeds that would taint the oil, so George hired a couple of high school athletes to help him with the hoeing. Up and down the rows they labored, keeping the plants weed-free and aerated. It was boring, no doubt, but the boys idolized Mr. McConnell and liked to work for him because, when he would call the end to the day's work, he would race them back to the barn, leaping fences and whooping for joy. Their boss was a slow and steady worker. Nothing seemed to wear him out.

The boys would get back to the barnyard and wash up at the livestock trough, marveling at the golden carp that lazily swam back and forth. The big fish ate the algae and kept the water from freezing in the winter, so the horses and milk cow could always get a drink. Mrs. McConnell would serve them all lemonade from a crock on the back stoop. They would thank her kindly, dropping their eyes and trying the whole time to ignore her "condition." It was impolite to stare at this woman who was in her last months of pregnancy, but the boys always watched for the light in Mr. McConnell's eyes when he looked at his wife. Each boy hoped some day to look at a girl that way. Before heading home, they would try to beat Mr. McConnell at horseshoes, but it was a lost cause. He was the county champion and could throw one resounding ringer after another—all the while with a big smile on his face and a lighted cigar clenched between his teeth. The boys admired this young couple something awful. They seemed to have the world on a string. They even owned a Model T, and the boys got a ride once in a while.

On Saturday afternoons in good weather, George, Lilah, and Helen took the car to Columbia City, bought some groceries, had a dish of ice cream or a piece of fresh strawberry pie in season at the drug store, and sometimes saw a silent film. All three liked to watch Mary Pickford's adventures on the silver screen while the man at the piano would pound out the musical score.

Helen was a likeable, bright child and was welcome in all the family households. Evan and Bess liked to play with her when she visited her grandparents. Evan set her high up on the back of a workhorse as he led the team home from the fields. He loved her happy spirit, sense of humor, and cute baby talk. Miriam relished the chance to take Helen in the buggy to see her friends. She would sometimes put Helen up on the counter in the store in Churubusco and have her do a little recitation or dance Lilah had taught her. She was Miriam's pride and joy. Helen also spent a good deal of time with her great-grandparents at the big brick house. Grandpapa was getting very old, but he was kind to her and loved to tell her stories of when he was a young man in the days of the pioneers. In the summers, JJ, the white-haired patriarch, would supervise the planning of Pence family reunions, which were always a wonderful success with up to 250 people attending. Due to his advancing age and because he had outlived his whole generation, he was always the center of attention at these gatherings, which suited him just fine. Helen was proud of this noble man, and she could tell her parents and grandparents felt the same, but he had suffered some sort of illness that had been causing him to steadily weaken, and he didn't tell her stories anymore. When she visited, she had to run and play very quietly, but he still would smile when she stood beside him—her hand on his knee.

The farm families in Whitley County were delighted when rural phone service reached their homes. The lines had been strung up and down the county roads, and the neighbors were connected like never before. Dave and Miriam shared a party line with neighbors, which meant that two rings was a call for Jim and his family up the road. A sequence of three close rings was a call for them. If Miriam wanted to use the phone to call Lilah and George, she picked up the receiver and listened for a second to make sure the line was clear. If she heard a conversation, phone etiquette required she must hang up gently, wait patiently for five or ten minutes, and then try the call again. If the line was clear, the operator, who was a neighbor farmwife who was paid to run the switchboard from her own home, would ask to whom she wished to speak and would plug in the wires accordingly. It was nothing short of a miracle. Miriam's voice traveled over a wire, and she was compelled to imagine what Lilah looked like on the other end.

Since phone calls were reserved for important messages instead of idle chatter,

Miriam always answered three rings of the phone with a vague sense of trepidation. Her instincts were right that chilly fall morning in September because it was Dave's sister Florence with the news that Father was gone. Alice and the doctor had worked to keep him comfortable in his old wicker chair both day and night into which he sank into his last sleep and passed peacefully into the world beyond.

Joseph J. Pence, the venerable old man, was laid to rest across the county road from the Blue River Church, which was overflowing with mourners at his funeral. The family had met to make arrangements to erect a large stone to commemorate his life, which had been a noble one. He was a true old settler, a man who would be missed because he was one of only a few left who could tell the whole story of life in the wilderness of northern Indiana. To report his passing to the community, the newspaper honored him with a long obituary which stated, "In politics he gave an unqualified allegiance to the Republican party. He was a man of excellent business judgment and sterling integrity, he being well-met by all who knew him, always having a kind word for a friend." To look at the vast fields of corn and the loitering cattle now, it was hard to imagine life as JJ knew it as a boy. Those days were long gone into the annals of time, and much of what he knew and experienced would be forgotten.

William Cullen Bryant had always been Father's favorite poet; he liked to read his work aloud to the family around the fireside in the evenings. Florence found the poem "Thanatopsis" marked with a red velvet bookmark on the walnut end table by his old chair, so Dave shared an excerpt of the poem in addition to the minister's traditional prayers at the funeral. The words seemed to encapsulate his long, eventful life and his passing:

"…Yet not to thine eternal resting-place
Shalt thou retire alone, nor couldst thou
wish couch more magnificent.
Thou shall lie down
With patriarchs of the infant world–
with kings,
The powerful of the earth—
the wise, the good,
Fair forms, and hoary seers of ages past,
All in one mighty sepulcher.

…So shalt thou rest—
and what if thou withdraw
In silence from the living, and no friend
Take note of thy departure?
All that breathe

Will share thy destiny. The gay will laugh
When thou art gone,
the solemn brood of care
Plod on, and each one as before will chase
His favorite phantom;
yet all these shall leave
Their mirth and their employments,
and shall come
And make their bed with thee.
As the long train
Of ages glides away, the sons of men—
The youth in life's fresh spring,
and he who goes
In the full strength of years,
matron and maid,
The speechless babe,
and the gray-headed man—
Shall one by one be gathered to thy side,
By those, who in their turn,
shall follow them.

So live,
that when thy summons comes to join
The innumerable caravan, which moves
To that mysterious realm,
where each shall take
His chamber in the silent halls of death,
Thou go not,
like the quarry-slave at night,
Scourged to his dungeon,

but, sustained and soothed
By an unfaltering trust,
approach thy grave
Like one who wraps the drapery of his
couch about him,
and lies down to pleasant dreams."

CHAPTER 35 1916

Lilah and George grieved for Father at home. Three days before JJ left the world, a new life had entered. Lilah gave birth, uneventfully this time, to a second daughter. They named her Marjory Geneva, and she was a lovely, round-eyed baby with a lock of blonde hair over her forehead and a little bow mouth. She was chubby and healthy, and George and Lilah rejoiced at their good fortune. George didn't get his boy, but Helen had turned out to be a good sport and a tomboy. He had taught her to catch fly balls with a mitt, and she played rough and tumble with her cousins, yelling until she was hoarse and had to be dosed with chamomile tea and honey. George wasn't timid to hold his daughter this time around, and he lifted the precious bundle and waltzed his new love around the room while Lilah watched from the bed, grinning at her husband's antics.

Helen loved her good-natured baby sister, who was a whole ten years younger, and pitched in to help with bathing and dressing duties. Helen insisted Marjory always wear a pretty lace cap on her head. She thought of her little sister as her pretty doll to dress and tuck in at night. Then, when Helen was done playing, she left Marjory to her own devices, putting her doll aside. Lilah spent lots of time going over Helen's lessons with her while Marjory sat on Helen's lap. Helen rode in the same horse-drawn school wagon that had delivered her mother to the nearest country school. On winter mornings, she and her schoolmates were chilled to the bone from riding in the old wagon. Helen had many friends in school and excelled in her studies. She wanted to emulate pretty Miss Harper, who had the responsibility for thirty-five pupils—all eight grades—and she taught all subjects to each grade and handled the big boys with ease. Helen believed that teaching would be the most wonderful profession a woman could choose.

In late September, George painstakingly harvested his first crop of mint. First, he mowed the plants down, trying not to disturb the roots. He ran a horse-drawn rake up and down his fields to mound the cuttings in neat rows to dry in the sun for a couple of days. After the rows were dry, he gathered the mint hay with an implement that chopped it and blew the small pieces into a wheeled tub. He processed the clippings by applying pressurized steam, which vaporized the mint oil from the leaf tissue. The resulting hot vapor condensed in a mint still. The lighter oil floated to the top of the water, and George dipped the oil into ten gallon galvanized steel cans for transport. The air for miles around carried the aroma of mint from George's distillery operation. He hauled the sloshing cans to the train station, and off they went to Chicago. Before long, true to his contract, a big check and a letter came personally from Charles Wrigley. George's mint oil proved to be of superior quality, and he was offered a contract to provide mint oil for the next year, promising big money from his unique crop. A pint of his Thorncreek Township mint oil would be used to flavor over 12,000 sticks of gum and would end up in every state in the Union. How about that? George's risk had paid off, and his future on this mucky soil was secure. Next spring, the perennial mint plants would emerge from the dark soil and grow even bigger and better. He might even get two cuttings of mint hay next summer. He planned to put in another unusual crop: onions. He just needed a couple of high school boys who didn't mind a few blisters on their hands and who would work and play side by side with him. This was his idea of 20th century farming.

CHAPTER 36   1917

It began as a vague ache that was most noticeable in the mornings upon rising, and, within months, Miriam felt a lump in her right breast.   In her years working with the women in the county, she had observed every malady that could affect the body. She had dealt effectively with many of them with help from Dr. Chase's medical book, and she had worked in concert with the local doctors to accomplish a number of full recoveries. Herbal treatments and good nursing care had helped Hilda recover from scarlet fever, and she attended Jane and her new baby for seventy-two hours as they both battled undiagnosed fevers to a successful outcome. Her reputation as a healer and able doctor's assistant had also caused many a farmer to call upon her when his mare was having trouble foaling or his workhorses had a contagion of one sort or another. She was never shy to suggest a farmer put down a contagious horse, if it was beyond treatment, and the level of respect they felt for her made these men accept her advice without question.

But there was one malady that she had never been able to cure. The very best doctors stood helpless before it: cancer. She had attended many women with cancers of the breast and womb, and it was a long road of pain and suffering until they were released to join their loved ones up above. Several of these unfortunate women were Pythian Sisters, but they had faced their fates with faith, strength, and uncommon courage.

She tried very hard to remain calm and quiet about her condition. She knew from her reading that there were big city doctors who could do major surgery to remove both breasts, but radical treatment did not substantially increase the woman's years of survival, and the surgery was debilitating. She knew God would give her some time—some short months of precious time—to keep on with her work, her friendships, her church responsibilities, and her dear family.

Miriam realized she had gained an inner peace in the last few years. Since her mother's death, she had resolved to remain aloof to the family drama that still swirled around the division of the Coulter farm. She did not need to be involved. Her brother Evan had passed away during all this turmoil, leaving his wife and three children without much financial backing. Sal and the children had gone back to her family, and Miriam thought that was for the best. Frank, John, and Margaret were the only three left to fuss over the spoils in the courts of the land, and they were getting too old for all this nonsense. She controlled her frustration and sorrow, and she held back from entering the fray. She was gratified to think she had done honor to her beloved Pa and Ma by the sort of life she had led. She would look forward to meeting them on the heavenly shores.

For now, she needed to turn her attention to Dave. She still loved him fiercely, and she wondered how he would get along without her. When it came down to the time when she could no longer hide the pain and had no choice but to tell him of her illness, she would encourage him to remarry—to find a woman who would be his helpmate. She had seen too many men spiral into destructive despair as widowers. Just last week, she and Dave were standing in the pine grove and saw their sad, pale, old neighbor—a man of former stellar qualities—drive his buggy past without even a look in their direction. He was bent over the reins, his clothing disheveled, his face a stubble of unkempt whiskers. He had lost his wife to a stroke only months before and was already showing signs of loneliness and physical and mental decay. She and Dave both halted, hands poised in greeting and lips ready to call out a hello, looked at one another with eyes of sadness and regret, and slowly lowered their hands. Instead of waving, they joined hands in understanding.

She was young, only fifty-two years old. Dave was young, too. He didn't need to run this place by himself. Jealousy of another woman taking her place would not even enter her mind. After her passing, he still had more than thirty years to live, if he was to live as long as his father. Lilah had her hands full with her two girls, George, and the farm. She couldn't be company for her father, even if she wanted to. Lilah would be hurt by a remarriage, but she would come to understand her father's need for companionship and help. But then, there was Evan.

Yes, Evan. She worried most about her smiling Irish son. He had married good-natured Bess, and she was tolerant of his lack of ambition. They were well-matched and so kind to Helen, though it didn't seem as if they had any desire for children of their own. He had continued to work for Dave and did a fair job with what he was asked to do. He seemed to have given up trying to please his father, who was certainly a perfectionist. Dave gave him all his farm papers and journals, but Miriam had seen them go into the backyard incinerator at their little cottage, unread.

She was not sure Evan could have read them, if he had tried. Bess dealt with all the important mail, and she was in charge of paying their bills. When Evan was little, Miriam had tried to help him with his schooling, but she noticed he reversed his letters, could not seem to memorize the sequence of the alphabet, and complained about his eyes when she would sit down with him to practice. She had recently read an Englishman's new theory of congenital word blindness. She wondered if that might have been what afflicted Evan and had caused him so much frustration and anger in school. The doctor had written a book about a case where a fourteen year old boy could do all other normal activities, but, for some reason, he couldn't be taught to read. The boy in the newspaper article had reminded her so much of her son and his struggles.

Evan seemed to have found what he wanted, though, and was satisfied to have a simple life with no frills. He did, still, count on Miriam to keep the peace between him and his father. She had always been a buffer, and, with her passing, he would find himself in direct conflict for the first time. If his dad remarried, that would be a terrible blow to Evan. The idea of her dear, sparkling-eyed son being hurt and heartbroken saddened her more than the cancer, more, almost, than leaving this world behind.

CHAPTER 37 1917

George was the proud owner of a Brownie box camera, and he brought it over to the Pence farm the next Sunday after church. It cost him a dollar new, fifteen cents additional for each roll of film. He insisted that the family go out in the yard to get a good image, and he summoned the hired man to run the camera. George steered each subject by the shoulders and positioned Bess, Evan, and Lilah in the back row, leaving room for himself next to Lilah. On the left-hand chair, he situated Miriam and plopped baby Marjory on her lap. Marjory was bright-eyed and happy, and Miriam fingered the satin ribbons on her pretty knitted cap. Marjory smiled a happy baby smile up in the face of her gray-haired grandmother and reached up to pinch her nose. Miriam hugged her close in response, unexpected tears welling up behind her wire-rimmed glasses.

George asked Dave to be seated in the other chair and to hold Helen in his lap. Helen was getting so big. She wore a white skirt, middy blouse, a blue sash, and a big white ribbon pinned on top of her head. She leaned awkwardly on her grandfather's lap. She didn't really fit there anymore and didn't quite know what to do with her long arms, so she tried her best to pose like Mary Pickford. Her hair was long, dark, and curled with a hot iron into ringlets. Miriam smiled to recall the times when she could easily lift Helen up to dance, recite, and sing on the counter at the general store. Helen's sweet baby voice had brought all the shoppers over to clap for her. She would be ready for high school before too long. Miriam hoped George would move his family to Columbia City in the winters so Helen could attend a more prestigious school. Lilah could join some clubs and those long winters on the farm would be replaced with dances, socials, and attendance at one of the big churches in town. George had mentioned the idea to her once, to see what she thought. Miriam thought it a brilliant idea, especially now.

She trusted Helen and Marjory would go to college and train for professions. They would be able to marry well and move into the mainstream of American life, instead of dedicating their lives to the land. The dreams she had for Lilah would come true in the next generation. Miriam could sense Evan standing behind her; today, his hair was combed and he was in his Sunday suit and tie. Lilah was to his left in a stylish striped skirt with an over-shirt and curled collar.

Dave could rely on this kindred spirit—this responsible daughter and her fine husband. Lilah would stay ever loyal to her dad, just as she had been from the day she was born.

As George fussed to make sure he could get everyone in the picture and to show the hired man just what to do to make the camera go, Miriam thought of her secret and looked over at Dave. He didn't care to have his picture taken, and always refused to smile. She had often chuckled to see him in photos: head turned to the side, his high forehead, ears forever sticking out, prominent nose, and deep-set eyes. After all these years, he was still her "chicken coop boy," and she decided that her last thoughts on this earth would be the magical moment when the luna moth descended upon them from the heavens and sealed their fate as man and wife and partners in this world, for better or for worse.

She knew worse was coming. Her illness would be difficult, but she could count on her Pythian Sisters to be at her side whenever she called, and they would personally conduct their beautiful graveside ritual. Six of her closest friends would bear flowers to decorate her grave near Pa and Ma. Most of the women had telephones, and a few had autos and sons to drive them over when she needed to call for help. She had a good doctor, Alice Williams, to tend her. She was glad to have a woman doctor—in fact, she wanted to be surrounded by women until the end. They would be her angels and usher her into the presence of God. She knew what was in store. She and death were well acquainted, and she had no fear of it.

And she had her trust in God. She thought back to her promise she had made at sixteen, to serve the greater community. She had been a pillar of strength to many and that was a comfort. She thought of dear Clover, buried now in the pasture that was her home, and of the side-saddle stored next to her empty stall in the new barn. She hoped Dave would pass that saddle on to Lilah as more of a relic than anything, but also as a memory of her independent spirit and his support of her over and above any other person in his life.

She thought of Pa: his beautiful voice, strong arms, rough hands, and tickling fingers. Later today, she would present Helen with the birdstone and the story to go with it. She thought of Ma and her peacocks. She smiled when she thought of Ma tending peacocks in Heaven, and little blonde Willie chasing them, trying to pull the feathers from their tails. Her faith told her she would be reunited with these loved ones soon, and the profound thought made her heart skip a beat.

She thought of how the world had turned so many times since her birth, bringing new ideas and inventions into little Whitley County each day, it seemed. She had lived to see the telegraph and now the telephone; the horse and buggy and now the horseless carriage; the kerosene lamp and now the electric bulb; the log cabin and now the lovely mansions in town. There were flying machines that would ply the air over Whitley County before too long. What marvels these all were—and so many more to come. Her lifetime had begun on the heels of a divisive war on American soil, and now another war threatened in Europe; but, overall, she had lived in a time of peace, idealism, and growing prosperity. She hoped and prayed that her grandchildren would live lives as fulfilling as hers had been, and that they would, above all, find love and raise good, strong, educated children in this land of opportunity.

She would face the pain and rely on God to help her through to the other side. She would instruct the doctor to give her laudanum, enough to dull her senses but not too much to keep her from saying the things she needed to say to her loved ones. When anyone entered her sickroom, she would summon every ounce of courage and show them what a God-fearing Hoosier woman was made of. Integrity, love of God, and respect for His power. Those principles and this family gathered about her would be her legacy to the world.

George finished his instructions to the hired man, grinned at everyone, and quickly took his place next to Lilah. The hired man held the camera waist-high, aimed it carefully, and, holding his mouth just so, turned the knob. Each family member, even Baby Marjory, heard the click that captured three generations—frozen in time.

Credits and Resources

I would like to thank the following for their help in the writing of this book:

Thomas Duncan for his constant encouragement

Anna Roth, fellow writer and astute reader, from Off the Beaten Path Bookstore, Steamboat Springs, CO

Jennie Lay from the Bud Werner Memorial Library, Steamboat Springs, CO

Tara, my fellow writer, in the November, 2011, NaNoWriMo.com challenge

Dr. Donald Gradeless for his dedication to Whitley County research

The Indiana Genealogical Society

Whitley County Historical Society

Marie Rathvon and Andrew Duncan for technical assistance

Non-Fiction Sources:

Counties of Whitley and Noble, Indiana: Historical and Biographical. Goodspeed/Blanchard; F.A. Bettey and Co, Publishers, Chicago; 1882.
(available in its entirety online at: family.gradeless.com/History_Whitley_County_1882.pdf)

Dr. Chase's Third, Last, and Complete Receipt Book and Household Physician; A.W. Chase, M.D.; F. B Dickerson and Co, Detroit; 1891.

Indiana: An Illustrated History, Patrick Joseph Furlong, Windsor Publications, Inc. 1985.

Whitley County Family History, Helen McConnell Alexander's personal memoirs, 1979.

Credits: Learn more about the literary references in this book:

"Wishing you a rainbow…" www.irishsayings.org

"O God, Our Help in Ages Past," Isaac Watts, 1719 paraphrase of Psalm 90; music: William Croft; listen at:
www.youtube.com/watch?v=dQmF1svW5Q

"Jesus, Keep Me Near the Cross," Fanny Crosby, blind poet, circa 1850. Listen at: www.elyrics.net

"What We Believe," www.merriamchapel.com

"May Love and Laughter Light Your Days," www.islandireland.com

"Where Did You Come From, Baby Dear?" George MacDonald, visionary Scottish poet; Youtube series: gmdinformation

"Thanatopsis," William Cullen Bryant 1794-1878; www.poetry-archive.com/b/thanatopsis.himl

For additional information, questions, or comments, please feel free to contact the author at sylduncan@hotmail.com